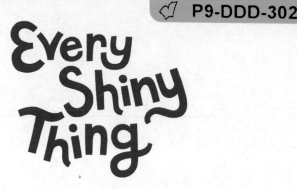
Every Shiny Thing

"Like a kaleidoscope, Lauren and Sierra's shifting perspectives will make you look at the world from different angles, transforming in unique and beautiful ways. This story shines."
—Lisa Graff, author of *Lost in the Sun*

"This should hit the mark for middle grade readers who enjoy life's complexities paired with the intrigue of secrecy."
—Erin E. Moulton, author of *Flutter*

"Thoughtful readers will find a lot to like here—sadness, suspense, even humor. They may even pause to consider their own privilege."
—*School Library Journal*

"Each character is well defined . . . Readers will hope for a better life for both girls. This middle grade novel will find a ready audience in most libraries."
—*Voices of Youth Advocates (VOYA) Magazine*

"Sierra's narrative, in poetry, captures her spare, cautious, and constrained life. Lauren's prose is rich and descriptive, much like her own experiences. Together, the contrasting narratives tell a touching story about friendship, loyalty, and resilience that will have lots of appeal."
—*Booklist*

"Two authors combine their efforts to relate the intertwined tales of a pair of young teens in trouble . . . Many of the complications of human behavior are on display here, some of them painful to navigate."
—*Kirkus Reviews*

Every Shiny Thing

CORDELIA JENSEN
and
LAURIE MORRISON

AMULET BOOKS
NEW YORK

The Library of Congress has cataloged the hardcover edition as follows:
Names: Morrison, Laurie, author. | Jensen, Cordelia, author.
Description: New York : Amulet Books, 2018. | Summary: Seventh-grader Lauren begins stealing to help children who, like her brother, are on the autism spectrum, and Sierra, in foster care in Lauren's neighborhood, fears she will enable Lauren's lawbreaking. Told half in prose, half in verse.
Identifiers: LCCN 2017032174 | ISBN 9781419728648 (hardback)
Subjects: | CYAC: Conduct of life--Fiction. | Stealing--Fiction. | Autism--Fiction. | Brothers and sisters--Fiction. | Foster children--Fiction. | Friendship--Fiction. | Family problems--Fiction. | BISAC: JUVENILE FICTION / Social Issues / Values & Virtues. | JUVENILE FICTION / Social Issues / Friendship. | JUVENILE FICTION / Social Issues / Special Needs.
Classification: LCC PZ7.1.M673 Eve 2018 | DDC [Fic]--dc23

Paperback ISBN 978-1-4197-3377-2

Text copyright © 2018 Cordelia Jensen and Laurie Morrison
Illustrations copyright © 2018 Kimberly Glyder
Book design by Alyssa Nassner

Printed and bound in U.S.A.
10 9 8 7 6 5 4 3 2 1

ABRAMS The Art of Books
195 Broadway, New York, NY 10007
abramsbooks.com

For Vermont College of Fine Arts—
the place that brought us together
and the people who've helped us grow

LAUREN

The Hardest Goodbye

There's nothing harder than saying goodbye to Ryan.

It was hard enough back in August, when Mom and Dad first took him to his new school. Back then, I knew I'd miss him. And I was afraid that this fancy therapeutic boarding school way far away in the middle of nowhere, North Carolina, wasn't the right place for him, even though Ry said he wanted to go, and Mom and Dad kept gushing about what a wonderful opportunity it was, and his old occupational therapist, Jenna, said you couldn't find a better school for a teen on the autism spectrum.

But saying goodbye today, at the end of Family Weekend? This was worse. Way, way worse. Because now that I've seen the place for myself and seen how Ryan is there, I'm not just *afraid* it isn't right. Now I *know* it's not.

It was awful. Really, it was. Not the kind of awful that would be obvious right away, if you weren't paying close attention. It's actually sort of beautiful, with purple-gray mountains in the distance and a long, winding driveway and super-green hills. The buildings are all new, with big windows and soft lights, and there are pretty wood stables with brown and black and reddish horses, and vegetable gardens with neat rows of kale and broccoli and beets.

But it's awful for *Ryan*.

Ryan's happiest at home, where he has his own calming corner set up in the basement, and his own, always-tuned piano in the living room, and his own fish tank to take care of.

At the school, they let him set up his keyboard and a teeny-tiny fish tank in his room . . . but still. It's nothing like the calming corner at home, which took ages to get just right. And he has to take piano lessons for his "arts component" even though he likes to play *his* way, just hearing the notes in his head, not reading music.

And he's supposed to help take care of horses and vegetables even though he doesn't like getting dirty. Horses and vegetables aren't "therapeutic" at all, when it comes to Ry. *That's* why he got so upset yesterday when he was taking us around to see the stables and gardens. This know-it-all occupational therapist named Scott said maybe Ryan needed some alone time in his room, since Family Weekend can be a big stressor for students who have just gotten used to their school routine. As if *we* were the reason he got overwhelmed. When really we're the ones who know how to help him the best.

I was sure Mom and Dad saw how wrong it all was, too. I was sure they were going to say something this morning, when we all went back to Ryan's room after breakfast. About how it was good that we'd given it a try, but this wasn't working, so we should just take Ryan home.

They looked at each other for an extra long time, and then Dad gave a tiny little nod, like he was telling Mom it was time. Time to say it.

Mom's eyes were a little teary, as if maybe she felt bad about how wrong they'd been to think Piedmont was a good idea in the first place. But then she reached into her giant bag and pulled out two wrapped, rectangular presents—one big and one little—and handed them to Ryan.

"What are these for?" Ryan asked.

"Dad and I wanted you to have something special," she said. She gave Ryan a wobbly smile, and her voice was way too cheerful. "For being so brave and independent."

"We're proud of you, buddy," Dad added. "Go on. Open them."

So Ryan tore the paper off the big one, and he let out a happy yell when he saw what it was: a MacBook Air. Then he opened the other one and yelled out again. The newest iPhone.

He yanked the computer out of its box first, and Dad recited the stats he'd learned at the Apple store, about how fast the processing speed was and how quickly YouTube videos were going to load.

I lowered myself down to sit on the edge of Ryan's school bed, which has a boring gray comforter because the bed's too small for the green one from home, and I tried to understand what was happening.

It's not like Mom and Dad have never bought us anything nice before. And Ry had told us a hundred times when the new iPhone was coming out, so it wasn't a secret that he wanted one. But they'd gotten him a phone *and* a laptop, when it wasn't even a holiday?

And once he opened his presents, we didn't talk about the smelly horses and muddy vegetable gardens, or how Scott the

OT is nowhere near as nice as Jenna, Ry's OT at home. We only talked about the apps Ryan wanted to download and a new music program he was going to set up on the computer.

Which was Mom and Dad's plan, probably. To distract Ryan with these shiny new electronics to make it easier when we left.

When it was time for us to go, Ryan walked us to our rental car. Dad said goodbye first. He leaned in close to whisper something I couldn't hear, and then he kissed Ry on the forehead. Then Mom clasped Ry's hand and rested her head on his shoulder for just a second, since he's taller than she is now. "I love you so much," she told him. "We'll miss you so much, honey."

When she pulled away, tears were streaming down her face. For a fraction of a second, I felt sorry for her, but *she's* the one who decided it was a good idea for Ryan to go to this terrible school, where he obviously doesn't belong. She and Dad both did.

Then Ry pressed his palm to mine, the way we always do instead of hugging.

"Bye, La," he said.

"Bye, Ry Guy," I said back, and I couldn't help it. I cried, too. It was too much, knowing he was about to go back into those too-new buildings with all of those people who think they understand him so much better than we do just because they're autism experts, when we're *Ryan* experts.

"I'm okay, La-La," Ryan told me. "I'm happy."

But I don't believe he's really happy. I mean, happy for a minute, because of Mom and Dad's guilt gifts? Maybe. But for-real happy? There's just no way.

The thing about Ry is, sometimes he goes along with things that make him feel awful because he wants to make other people feel good, and then it all gets to be too much, and he melts down. Like how he came along to Visiting Day at my camp over the summer and went to lunch in the loud cafeteria with fluorescent lights and then came into my crowded cabin that stank of Addie Lester's peach body lotion. Noises and lights and smells are so intense for him that he probably felt like someone was scratching their fingernails down a blackboard one millimeter from his eardrum while shining a giant searchlight straight into his eyes and squirting skunk spray up his nostrils. But he did it all because he thought it was important to me.

So now he might just be sticking out boarding school because he thinks it's important to Mom and Dad. And there'll be nobody around but Scott the Smug OT to comfort him when it's all too much to stick out.

"You *sure* you're okay?" I asked him. "You don't want to come home?"

He tapped his fingertips against mine, twice, and then took his hand away. "I'm going to go to a good college," he said. "I'm going to learn so much."

That's what convinced him that the Piedmont Therapeutic Boarding School was a good idea. Mom took him to the University of Pennsylvania a lot last year to see lectures and tour the archaeology museum. He wants to go there for college someday, so he can listen to all the history and science lectures he wants and visit the Egyptian exhibit anytime. Mom says, now that Ry's fourteen, they've hit their homeschooling limit, and he needs real professionals to push him so he can "reach his academic potential."

But she could hire tutors who could challenge him in subjects that she can't. And then he could learn enough to get ready for college and still live at home with us. In what universe is dumping him at Piedmont better than that?

And . . . OK. Here is the very worst thing. Now that we've just left him at his school with the shiny new electronics that won't fix anything and horses I know he doesn't want to clean up after and gross kale plants I know he doesn't want to water and piano lessons I know he must hate, there's a terrible, terrible thought that I can't push away any longer:

What if it's not that Mom and Ry reached the limit of how much he could learn with her homeschooling him?

What if Mom and Dad have reached their *Ryan* limit, and they've decided our lives would be easier without him?

SIERRA

Out of Body

Mom hugs me hard,
    says she'll be home soon.

Her eyes swollen,
      she whispers,

"Don't worry,
      my baby girl."

She doesn't say goodbye,
    so I don't either.

As one cop car
    takes her away,

my heart stays stuck
        in the spot
     she left behind
my body
     steps into another cop car
        a lady cop plugs in the address.

Even as she walks me
to Cassidy's front door,
my heart stays frozen.

It might never leave
that parking lot.

Not Until

"Happy birthday, hon,"
        Cassidy's mom, Lena,
                my mom's best friend,
pulls me in.
The smell of her day-drinking
wakes me up.

As a rule: She allows herself just one
                before the bus comes to deliver:

Cassidy,
the twins,
and then the older girls
Michelle,
Dawn,

                all back home.

Lena and I walk together to the bus stop.

"Something I know about your mom is, she loves you more
    than anything."

I don't want to cry anymore, so I focus
on stepping over the cracks in the sidewalk.

If she loves me so much, why didn't she listen to me?
Why doesn't she ever listen to me?
I want to ask.

Cassidy and her sisters bound off the bus.
At first, Cassidy's not surprised to see me.
Not until she sees my face.

And all my tears
painted there.

Won't Fit

Lena tells Cassidy's oldest sister, Dawn, to run to the
     mini-mart.

She sticks candles in my favorite kind of Tastykake.
A puffy pink Snowball.

Thirteen candles won't fit.
Lena settles on three.

They all sing happy birthday to me,
but just hearing the song makes me feel

swollen,
sick.

Counting

Mom uses her one phone call
to ask for bail money
from Lena.
I count what's in my wallet.
$11.

Mom uses her one phone call
to ask Lena
to keep me
until she can get out.

My fingers, uncrossed, cross.

Promises

"It'll be fun, you can sleep next to me."
Cassidy smiles,
showing her crisscrossed teeth,
tapping the bed next to her.

"Michelle sleeps there," I say.

Usually, on sleepovers, we just drag
sleeping bags into their den.

"We'll make her sleep with the twins!"
she giggles.
Mischief creeping in
to her yellow-green eyes.

Trying to laugh with her feels like trying to believe
Mom
      every time she says
      she will get sober
      things will be different.
            A new apartment.
            A new pet.
            A new job.

"It will be so fun," I laugh with Cassidy, toss a pillow
      at her.

Getting Ready

The morning,
>> menthol in hand,
>> one twin on her lap,
>> cereal bowls crowding the table,

Lena tells me—
She doesn't have bail money.
Or enough to keep me
long.

But she says—the arrest was just for
disorderly conduct & resisting arrest.
Usually those sentences
are
short.

"Unless—"
Something passes over her face,
but she drags her cigarette,
stuffs it back down.

I want to ask her if she knows where I'll go.
But, instead, I get ready for school.
Borrow Michelle's clothes, tiny Cassidy's too small for me.

Close my eyes, see Mom handing me lunch money.
Tell myself she will make bail from someone else.
She will get me back.

She has to.

Practice problems in my head.
It's Wednesday, and there's a big math test.

Moving Sideways

Lena drives us to school,
to make sure I'm OK.
Walks us in.
From the car to school,
Cassidy whispers:

> she will convince her mom to keep me as long as I need,
> she will snag a mattress from her neighbor,
> she will start saving some of her food for me.

I nod at all her plans.

But when we get to school,
instead of letting me go forward
to math for my test,
the school counselor
is there waiting for me.
And someone else I don't know.
A heavyset woman with glasses.

Moving me sideways.

They need to speak to me

right away.

Lena clasps my hand
I have no choice but   to follow.

LAUREN

What Really Matters

I followed Mom and Dad through the Asheville airport, barely looking up. Without Ryan, nobody pointed out which planes were Airbus A320s or Boeing 767s. Mom made a big thing of taking the middle seat on the plane and giving me the window. With only three of us, we fit on one side of the aisle. No need to split up two and two.

I tried to talk to Mom and Dad once the plane took off. I told them all the ways the school is wrong for Ryan, and at first, I thought I was getting through to them. Mom looked like she might start crying again, and even Dad blinked too many times and kept twisting his wedding ring around and around on his finger, as if he might crack, too, if he didn't focus all his attention on that shiny gold band.

But then Dad laced his big fingers through Mom's thinner ones, and Mom reached over to squeeze my hand, too.

"We know this is so hard, honey," she said. "But this is going to be so good for Ryan."

And then Dad started in with his lawyer routine. Laying out all the evidence in favor of Piedmont in his calm, definite voice.

"Piedmont has autistic adults on the board who consult on all their therapies," he said. "It's so much more progressive than the Keller School was. So much more tuned in to what Ryan needs."

And, OK, Piedmont's not as bad as Keller, the school near our house for kids with learning differences where Ryan went the year before last. At Keller, they tried to force him to make eye contact and stop stimming, which is what it's called when he rubs the fabric of his T-shirts and flicks his fingers to calm himself down when things are hard. When he went there, he was quiet and sad and had more meltdowns than he'd ever had before, until Mom and Dad pulled him out and found Jenna, who appreciates all the things he's good at and doesn't try to change him.

But just because Piedmont's better than Keller was, that doesn't make it *right*.

"We're so lucky we can afford this kind of opportunity for Ryan," Dad added.

Then Mom chimed in. "And you know Ry wants to be around other teens he can relate to."

Which he did say before he left in August. But then he barely even talked to any other students the entire time we were there.

"Sweetheart, you know this is what we decided as a family," Dad said.

As if *I* had any choice in the matter. As if my vote counts at all.

The flight attendant walked by and smiled as she looked at us. Mom, Dad, and me, holding one another's hands as we sat on one side of the aisle while Ryan was back in North

Carolina, all alone. The flight attendant probably assumed we were a happy family of three. She didn't have any idea at all. The whole thing was just so *wrong*.

So I yanked my hand out of Mom's grip and turned toward the window, watching the North Carolina mountains fade into the distance as the plane took us farther and farther away from Ry.

Back at home this morning, there were two rectangular presents at my place at the kitchen table—one big, one little. I didn't have to open them up to know what they were.

"We're proud of *you*, too, Laur," Dad said. "We know none of this is easy."

But somehow fancy new stuff is supposed to help?

"Now you have the same phone Audrey does!" Mom said. "And a fast new computer for your schoolwork."

They were both looking at me, their faces so cheerful. So sure that—*poof!*—a new phone and laptop would make me forget how terrible it was to leave Ry.

I left the presents where they were and grabbed a bagel.

"I'm ready to go to school," I told Mom. "Can you take me now?"

She'd said I could go late, since we hadn't gotten home from North Carolina until after ten. But I had no desire to stay in our too-clean, too-quiet, Ryan-free house with that terrible thought blaring louder and longer in my head, like when Ryan pushes one of the pedals on the piano to make a note ring out.

I missed the bus, but Mom dropped me off before advisory was over. I took a seat next to Audrey, who turned to a new piece of loose-leaf in her science binder and scribbled a note. *How was the school? You feel better now??*

I pressed my top and bottom teeth together, hard, so I wouldn't scream. Audrey's just so completely sure that my parents are right. That going to Piedmont's this amazing, exciting opportunity and it's just so completely awesome that Ryan can do it.

I didn't write her a note back, because there wasn't any point. When Ryan first left, I tried to tell her why I was worried, but she didn't listen at all. She kept saying, "Didn't Ryan say he wanted to go?" and, "Look, the website says they have a concert piano!" and, "I bet once you see it for yourself when you visit, you'll feel better about everything."

And that was wrong, wrong, wrong. I don't feel better at all.

Ms. Meadows stopped what she was saying to the group and smiled at me. "Morning, Lauren. We're just going over how we'll choose our student government rep."

Audrey pointed to her note with the top of her pen, and I managed a shrug.

"I can only nominate one student to be a representative, and it's a big responsibility," Ms. Meadows said. "But raise your hand if you're interested, and I'll talk to each of you over the next couple of days before I make my recommendation."

Audrey glanced at me as her hand shot up. We'd both done student government in sixth grade, but we weren't in the same advisory then. Ms. Meadows couldn't choose both of us now.

Three other kids raised their hands, too, but I kept mine down. Audrey's dark brown eyes went from nervous to confused, and then she stuck out her chin. That's what she does when she's annoyed.

We always used to go for all the same things, Audrey and me. Sometimes I think she isn't sure something's worth having if I don't want it, too. It's just . . . student government was important to me last year, but all we did was plan the themes for dances and organize bake sales so we could pay for real DJs instead of having high school students do it. Everybody got so worked up choosing between an outer space theme or a winter wonderland, but nothing we did really *mattered*.

"Terrific," Ms. Meadows said after she'd written down names. "And I'm also hoping one of you might be willing to be our Worship and Ministry rep."

Everyone looked down at their desks. Nobody *ever* volunteered for Worship and Ministry. Nobody Audrey and I were friends with, anyway.

"Mr. Ellis is advising this year, and he has a lot of exciting ideas! He wants to have the first meeting during lunch today."

Mr. Ellis teaches history, and he's new and young and funny. That was a good start but probably not enough to convince anybody, and Ms. Meadows knew it.

"It's a very important job," she went on. "This semester we're focusing on the Quaker testimony of simplicity, and the Worship and Ministry group will help us figure out how to make simplicity meaningful."

"Simplicity!" Max Sherman pumped his fist. "Woo-hoo, my favorite SPICE!"

The other guys all laughed.

SPICES is the word we learned back in lower school to remember the Quaker ideas we're all supposed to follow, since we go to a Quaker school. Simplicity, peace, integrity, community, equality, stewardship.

"Does that mean you're volunteering, Max?" Ms. Meadows asked.

Max shook his head so hard, I was surprised his Phillies hat didn't go flying. "No way. Sorry."

Ms. Meadows sighed. "Well, I won't force anyone. But if any of you change your mind . . ."

I thought of those two rectangular boxes waiting for me on the kitchen table at home. Somebody needed to teach my *parents* about simplicity.

"I'll do it," I said.

Audrey's mouth fell halfway open.

"Thank you, Lauren," Ms. Meadows said. "I'm sure Mr. Ellis will be thrilled to have you."

Then she changed the subject right away, probably so I couldn't take it back.

On the way out of advisory, Audrey cornered me. "Worship and Ministry club? Really? What's going on with you today? Are you OK?" She tapped the toe of one of her brand-new gray lace-up boots against the floor, waiting for me to answer.

But I had no idea what to say to any of those questions, so I shrugged again and headed to first period.

There should have been twelve kids in Worship and Ministry. One kid per advisory, three advisories per grade, four grades in middle school: fifth, sixth, seventh, and eighth. But only four people had signed up. Me, another seventh grader named Mariah, and two guys: Jake, who's in eighth grade, and Gordy, who's in sixth.

I took the seat next to Mariah. Her bangs are dyed neon blue, and she was wearing a T-shirt with a rip down the back and safety pins holding it together. I've gone to school with Mariah since kindergarten, but I've barely talked to her since, like, second grade.

"I like your hair," I told her.

Plenty of people tint the ends of their hair pink or red or purple or just dye streaks in the front, but nobody else in our grade has hair as bright as Mariah's. The first day of school, Audrey whispered that Mariah looked like a Smurf and that she could be pretty if she'd stop trying so hard to look weird. But what's wrong with trying to be a little bit different?

Mr. Ellis started the meeting. "I want to thank you all for giving up your lunchtime. I hear we have some Worship and Ministry veterans here." He paused to look at Jake and Mariah. "And some new volunteers, too. We've got a big job, people. Let's get going."

He started by asking us all what we thought of when we heard the word *simplicity*. I was sitting the closest to him, so I was up first.

I thought of that shiny new laptop. The shiny new phone. Audrey's shiny new boots. The shiny new cars that my parents drive and that all my friends' parents do, too.

"Um . . . I guess simplicity means not getting too wrapped up in material possessions. Like, not thinking that the most important thing in the world is whether you have the newest iPhone or brand-new shoes and clothes when that stuff maybe makes you feel good for a little while, but there are so many people who don't even have the things they need."

I was thinking about how Ryan's old occupational therapist, Jenna, works with people who can pay for their treatments, like us, and other families who can't. I used to go with Mom to pick Ry up from OT sometimes, and one time, he and two other kids were playing Jenga together. One of them was a girl with a puffy ponytail and oversized sweats. She looked about my age, and she was kneeling in front of the game, rocking back and forth. I could see in her face how hard she was fighting to keep herself calm. But then Ryan took a turn, and he must have taken the block she wanted to move, because she got upset and kept slamming her fists against the floor.

The girl wasn't there the next time Ryan had a social skills session, so I asked Jenna where she was.

"Hailey?" Jenna said. "Unfortunately, some of my clients can't come as often as Ryan. Some of their parents have to work multiple jobs, and they just can't get here more than once every week or two."

"But you do sessions at people's houses," I said, because she came to our house a lot. She helped us get the calming space in the basement just right, with low lighting and Ryan's fish tank to take care of and his keyboard to play.

Jenna and Mom exchanged a look.

"Lauren, honey, you know every kid on the spectrum is different. And every family is different, too," Mom said.

I thought that's all I was going to get, but then Jenna said, "The truth is, sessions are expensive. Insurance doesn't always cover the kind of therapy I do, and I have to charge even more when I go into families' homes."

Now everybody was still looking at me, in case I wasn't done talking about simplicity, and I was getting worked up remembering what Jenna had told me, because how unfair is that? That Ryan could have better treatment than other people just because Mom and Dad could pay for it and Mom didn't have to work? And if sessions at people's houses cost more than sessions at the OT center, I can't even imagine how much they're paying for Ryan to live at Piedmont, where they have OTs around all the time.

We're so lucky we can afford this opportunity for Ryan. That's what Mom and Dad had told me on the plane.

"I just think people at our school . . . we could really do something good," I said. "So many of us have so much. We could really help people who don't have enough."

Mr. Ellis smiled. "You're so right, Lauren. It sounds like you have a strong sense of social responsibility. With that kind of passion, we can really make a difference."

If Mr. Ellis says I'm right, then I must be. He did the Peace Corps for two years and then taught in a poor school in Northeast Philly before he came here. And Mariah, Jake, and Gordy all nodded like it was really something special, what I'd said.

In that moment, I felt better than I had in ages—since before Ryan went away.

And that's when I got the idea.

SIERRA

Crowding

Lena waves her girls to class,
keeps my hand.

We crowd into the office.

"Good morning. I'm Maude.
I'm with Child Protective Services."

I know what CPS is.
It's the organization that splits you
from your parents.
It's what the counselor threatened Mom with
last spring, when I skipped
so many days.

"Unfortunately, because your dad is in jail already,
and with your mom's arrest
combined with her DUI prior,
and on account of how you don't have other family members
  who could take you—"

"Did you try Uncle Mac?"
Mom's brother in Florida she hasn't spoken to in years.
"Unfortunately, he's very busy with his job and his kids."
Nan, already dead.
Dad's family, addicts.

"Seventy-two hours and then we will go to court,
it will all be more settled then."

I look to Lena.
She twitches her hands, like
she needs a cigarette.
"I can keep her that long—"

"Very well," says Maude.
Gives her some paperwork.

                    "So Mom could be back in a few days?"
Maude and the school counselor look at each other.
Then back at me.

                    "Anything's possible, Sierra."
She says she'll see us in court.

I close my eyes
and imagine myself surrounded
by the luckiest color, green.

Collide-o-scope

I always thought Mom was saying *collide-o-scope*.
She would say:
Sierra—
red's for love,
yellow for friendship,
blue for the sad kept inside of you,
green for those lucky days,
orange, the anger.
She said whichever
showed the most swirls
as they spun   and shook
            and shaped one another
was your day's fortune.
Sometimes her breath heavy with wine,
sometimes toothpaste fresh,
either way, curled to me,
asking me always
about the colors I see.

Rushing

After school,
Lena and I stop by the room Mom's been renting
so I can grab some stuff.
Pack quickly but make sure to grab
the kaleidoscope.
Back outside, I notice
someone's littered where
Mom tried to plant a garden
last spring.

I bend to pick up the trash but—

the lady who rented us the room
runs out,
yells at us, saying the rent's overdue.

Lena yells back a quick sorry,
"In a rush!"
Hurries me back to the car.

Impression

Seventy-two hours of pillow fights, TV binges, dance-offs
              Then—
              I have to—
Maude arrives, says Mom is still in jail.
"Pack up."
I tell Cassidy
I'll be back soon.
She tells me a dirty knock-knock joke,
says I should memorize it,
in case I need to make a good impression.

Maude sighs, says we have to go.
Cassidy gives me a hug
and a handshake,
when I open up my palm
I see she's given me
her last stick of gum.

On the Way

I was named for Sierra Road,
a big house there
Mom always wanted to be
ours.

Mom said
on the way to my birthday disaster
that she was going to get out of that room rental
that she got a raise at Wawa
we were going to move into
a new apartment development.
We'd lived in three of them
before.
This new one was called
Brighton Acres.
This one had a pool,
Mom said.
It was closer to the mall,
Mom said.

On the way to court,
just past the Wawa where Mom was working,
I spot the apartments.

Maude says they have some excellent foster parents lined up
for me.

I want to yell,
Let me out here.

I want to run
across the highway,
    dodge cars,
        go to the place
        where Mom and I were supposed to live

together, next.

Safety

At court,
I have a "child advocacy" lawyer.
She asks me a bunch of questions
about Mom and my life with her.

>How often she held a job.
>How often I skipped school.
>How often she was evicted.

Because she's a lawyer
I'm scared to lie
though most of me wants to.

They say
I'll be going
somewhere safe.

>But strangers aren't safe.

CPS says they're protecting you
but they're taking you from the people
who love you.

Mom's red love for me
fierce as
bear to cub.

Even though I had to tell the truth
answering those terrible questions

I know,
I know

she will
do everything she can
to get me back.

Proceedings

I see Mom on video.
She's watching the proceedings.

They say to get me back
she needs to follow the guidelines on the
Child Permanency Plan.

Once out of jail,
she needs to stay sober,
secure housing, a job.

I want to dive into the video,
tell her she can do it.

I need her to do it.

The caseworker congratulates me,

says I couldn't have asked

for a better foster home.
Says they   are experienced foster parents,
                   live in one of the nicest neighborhoods in
                        Philadelphia,
                   can afford to send me to private school.

I'm supposed to be happy about this?

I don't want to look at them,
my eyes glued to hers in the screen.

The foster parents are waving, smiling at me.

Him white, her black.

Nan would've said
something rude about it,
but she was so old-school,
Mom would say
you love who you love.

But they also look too old
to be taking in kids.

Their names are Anne and Carl,
both so tall.

I come from short people
with small hands.

They both try to take one of mine

like I'm a little kid.

We wade through the courtroom

    a sea of eyes

    fluorescent lights

    tissues, coughs, grunts.

I want to cry out to Mom to save me,
these people trying to hold my hand

no different than anyone

all of us

strangers
in a crowd.

Drive

Their car's bumper sticker reads:
ENCOURAGE YOUR HOPES
NOT YOUR FEARS
The car's old,
like them.
They live in Mt. Airy,
      the Northwest part of Philly.
      Driving through once,
      Nan told me Mt. Airy's for
      the hippies and the gays.
      Mom told her to be quiet,
      Nan hissed at her like a cat.

Now, down Germantown Avenue,
      Anne asks so many questions,
      Carl tells me about the school.
      Quaker, private.

I don't answer I
listen to my old iPod mini
Dad gave me a week after Christmas
a few Christmases ago
said he was waiting to make it more
of a surprise that way. He filled it
with our favorite movie theme songs.

I have his big UNCLE AL'S BAR & GRILL T-shirt on
and Mom's old plastic red ring.
They can take me
to wherever they live
but they can't make me

theirs.

The Sad in Me

The house is stone
all wood floor and creaks,
no carpet.
Mom would say looks like ghosts
live in the closets.
Dad would ask for the TV.
Anne shows me her craft table.
She makes jewelry, she says.
Silvers, golds blink from the table.
Anne says
they'll paint my room
in colors I like.
Yellows, reds, greens, blues.
She won't stop asking so
I tell her blue.
For the sad in me rising
swirling
to the top.

Staying Packed

Their stringy dog, Seeger,
bounds up to me, kisses my face.
I can't help but laugh
as much as I try to hold it in.
He smells like he needs a bath—

Upstairs, tell him to scram, need to unpack.
Thing is
though
he doesn't.
Thing is
though
I keep everything packed.

Except my kaleidoscope,
place it on the dark wood nightstand. Alone.

Sit on the cold, hardwood floor
pet Seeger's soft ears
think about Mitzi, Mr. Little, Cameron,
all those animals we've had and left,
one carpeted apartment to the next.
Wonder if we would've gotten another one,
when we moved to Brighton.

Maybe if Mom gets me back,
we will still move there.
Get some other animal.

For now, I'll live out of Nan's old suitcase.

Seeger sighs, falls asleep, head on my knee.

Into the Air

I hear them:
> Anne says I need time to settle in
> Carl says I need to get out   into the air.

> He wins.

He doesn't give me a choice—

"Let's go to the woods, put on your sturdiest shoes."

I look at what I have: two pairs of sneakers and some old
    sandals.

I put on the dirtier ones. The ones my mom just said I need
    to take better care of—

> Think of the last time I was ever in the woods.
> > Once, with Nan and her fisherman boyfriend.
> > They got drunk, I played with my Barbies

> pretended they were lost.

The Woods

There is a patch of woods
a few blocks
from their house.
Carl says
          sitting, walking, being
          in nature
               and just breathing
helps him feel strong
when he's sad, angry.

I look up at the colorful trees
the sun streaming through.
It's pretty but
I'm not sure what the view can do
to help me with Mom.

He tells me to practice deep breaths.
Inhale, exhale
gentle
as a leaf
in a breeze.
My breath stays shallow.
My mind only sees Mom in a cell.
Mom without me.

We loop back.

On the way, Carl says there's a room near mine
       I shouldn't go in,
that Anne'll get to crying and
Seeger'll run in and won't come out.
To be careful.

The leaves pulse red, orange.
My breath only gets shallower, faster.

Secret Room

Carl and Anne do yard work.
Anne says I should settle into
        my space.

What's the point?
I can't be settled without Mom.

Instead—

      I sneak into the secret room.

The room's set up for a girl.
      Not a girl like me.
      Pink curtains, unicorns, dress-ups.
           Shivers run through me.
           Cassidy would say it was creepy.
I look out the secret room's window.
Red, green, gold leaves fly,   through the air
           spiraling, spinning.
I jump.
In the window across, a girl from the house next door's
   looking right back.
Long brown hair, she's opening her window.
           To talk to me?
Like leaves,   I swirl around, make sure I close
   that door   back tight.

LAUREN

The Scheme Team

The deal is, yes, I do sort of need a new laptop for school, since I cracked the screen on my old one, and it was getting pretty slow. But do I need the thousand-dollar-plus MacBook Air Mom and Dad bought me? Definitely no. Plenty of people just have a netbook, which only costs a few hundred bucks.

So my idea was:

Step 1: Take back the Mac.
Step 2: Buy a netbook.
Step 3: Give the leftover money to Ryan's old OT, Jenna, to use for extra sessions with that girl Hailey and other patients who need them.

Not as good as getting Ry home from Piedmont, but at least it would be *something*.

Mom and Dad would notice I had a different computer, obviously. And when they did, I'd explain what I'd done and say sorry for going behind their backs, but it would be too late for them to do anything about it. "Easier to ask for forgiveness than permission," or whatever that expression is. Aunt Jill used to say it when she picked me up from school, because Mom was busy, and took me for ice cream even though it might spoil my dinner.

The laptop was still all sealed up in its box, so I thought I could take it back to the Apple store in Center City and ask for a refund. But it turns out that was wrong. I looked up returns online, and they'd only put the cost back onto Dad's credit card, which wouldn't help anybody at all.

So at dinner, I tried the honest approach. Dad was still at work, but Mom and I sat down at the kitchen table with tacos.

"With Ryan away . . ." Mom said, and then paused for so long, I thought she might not finish her sentence. "I have all this extra time I'm not sure what to do with. I thought I'd try a new recipe."

She looked away from me and sniffled a little, but it's because of her that he's gone. *She's* the one who heard about Piedmont and convinced Ry it would be good for him.

"The food looks good," I told her, and I took a deep breath. "Hey, so, about my laptop."

Her face lit up brighter than when I told her I made the A team for field hockey, I swear. "Can you believe how light it is? And so fast. Did you know Dad got me one, too? I just love mine."

I took a bite of bean and squash taco, which had a lot more spice and tang than anything Ryan would eat.

"Well, I was actually thinking I'd maybe like one of those netbooks instead."

She leaned her head back, as if she might understand what I'd just said if she could look at me from a little bit farther away. I guess that didn't work, though.

"Why?" she asked.

Then she spooned some guacamole onto her taco and held the bowl out to me, but I shook my head. She never would have made guacamole like that before. It had chunks of tomato and onion, which would freak Ryan out. He hates different textures mixed together.

"It's just . . . netbooks do everything I need."

Mom gave me the disappointed frown she used to save for when I complained about something I didn't get to do because of Ryan.

"Doesn't the Mac do everything you need, too?"

I fought the automatic awfulness that always used to rise in my gut when I did something to deserve that frown. It doesn't mean the same thing anymore.

"Well, yeah," I admitted. "But, you know, netbooks are a lot cheaper."

Mom reached over to pat my hand. "You don't need to worry about that, hon."

"But . . . I mean, don't you ever think about what that extra money could do for some people?"

She gave my hand a squeeze. "Of course I do. But, sweetheart, you've sacrificed a lot over the past few years. You deserve some nice things."

But what have I sacrificed, really?

Sometimes nobody could come to my field hockey or softball games last year because Dad was still at work and Mom was busy taking Ryan to a homeschooled-kids activity in the city. But Audrey's mom always sent my parents pictures, and Ry always stuck a good-luck note on my bedroom door—before every single game.

And, yes. One time when Audrey and our other friend Emma slept over, we snuck downstairs to watch a movie really late at night, and Ryan ran down the stairs wearing his favorite Batman pajamas, which didn't even come all the way down to his ankles anymore. "Mom! Dad! Lauren's down here watching TV even though it's lights-out time!" he yelled.

And Emma sat there at the edge of the couch with her eyes wide and her mouth half-open as Ryan kept shouting, "This isn't fair! This is against the rules!" And I never really wanted to invite her over again after that.

But it was my fault, really. I'm the one who broke a rule because I didn't want to admit that I wasn't supposed to be downstairs watching TV that late, and I know how much Ry hates it when people don't follow rules.

And OK, we usually went to the aquarium in Camden when we had family days, since Ry was comfortable there and we knew exactly what time to arrive to avoid the crowds. And sometimes I wanted to go to the zoo or the movies or a Phillies game instead, and I didn't get to. But does that somehow mean I deserve a shiny new laptop, just because I spent a lot of Saturdays looking at sharks and jellyfish and hippos?

Before I could figure out what to say, Mom stood up, leaving a guacamole-covered taco on her plate. "Speaking of nice things, I almost forgot!"

She walked out to the front hallway and came back with two bags: one from Lucky Jeans and the other from Urban Outfitters.

"We barely had time for back-to-school shopping this year. I picked you up a few new odds and ends."

I peeked inside the bags and pulled away the tissue paper. A pair of jeans from Lucky and two shirts and a sweater from Urban Outfitters.

"Those are the stores you wanted me to take you to last spring, right?" she asked. "Did I go to the right ones?"

The few bites of taco I'd eaten sank to the bottom of my stomach as I remembered the weekend before the spring dance last year. I'd wanted a new shirt and jeans for the dance because Audrey had gotten a new outfit, and I got mad when Mom couldn't take me shopping because she'd scheduled an extra OT session for Ryan.

I picked up a purple scoop-neck shirt.

"Pretty, right? Do you like it?" Mom asked.

Audrey has the same exact one in blue. The first time she wore it to school, three people complimented it before we even got to advisory.

Mom was smiling all the way up to her eyes. She *never* used to look at me that way—so hopeful and . . . focused. There were always five hundred distractions.

I was getting all these things I'd wanted so much last year: Mom's attention, new clothes from my favorite stores, and a break from eating the same four or five meals we always had. But none of it felt right at all.

"Really pretty," I agreed.

I was afraid I might cry again if I said anything more.

On Saturday morning, I was using my new Mac to start my history essay comparing the Great Depression to the financial crisis of 2008. I didn't want to disappoint Mr. Ellis—not after the way he'd looked at me at Worship and Ministry. But I couldn't come up with anything smart.

I kept checking my new phone for a video message from Ry. He sent me tons when I was at camp over the summer, so I've been making them for him a couple of times a week since he left for school. At first, he always sent one back right away. But now he keeps taking longer and longer to reply.

Mom said she just talked to him while I was at school yesterday, and he was excited about a project he and some other kids were doing with a science teacher, something about calculating the optimal percentage of nitrogen-rich raw materials they should put into their school compost piles. But, seriously, compost? I can't believe Ryan could possibly be excited about something as gross and smelly as compost piles full of people's half-eaten, rotting food.

And Mom said Ry had sent me so many messages over the summer because he was home without much going on, and the fact that he isn't sending as many now is a good sign because it means he's busy at school.

But I'm not so sure. Because what if he's just faking being OK, and he knows he couldn't fake it with me?

I went back to my document, typed a sentence, deleted it, and looked out my window, as if I'd find a decent thesis statement dangling next to the red and yellow leaves on the tree branch that waved up and down in the breeze.

Instead, there was a girl around my age, with straight blond hair, looking out the window that's always dark. *Amy's window*, Mom and Dad call it. Anne and Carl have taken in kids before—a little boy last year and an even littler boy the year before that. But never a girl, until now.

I tried to smile at the girl, but she didn't see me. I pulled open my sticky window, and her eyes widened when it creaked. Then—*poof!* She was gone. As if I'd spooked her.

I wanted to know her story. And how long she was going to live next door, and if maybe she'd start going to my school, like the little boys had. I could hear Anne and Carl in the yard. They'd probably invite me in to meet her if I went out to say hi.

My phone buzzed with a text from Audrey, asking if I'd meet her at Starbucks.

Need some Scheme Team time! she said.

The Scheme Team is what Audrey's dad started calling us when we were little because we always came up with big plans together. Some of our plans didn't exactly work, like our attempt to start a cooking camp for preschoolers in Audrey's kitchen when we were ten, or the time we constructed a miniature obstacle course on Audrey's driveway and invited all the kids on her street to enter a Hamster and Guinea Pig Obstacle Course Race for a five-dollar entry fee. But we pulled off a neighborhood talent show the summer before fifth grade and got eight of our friends to dress up in *The Wizard of Oz* costumes last Halloween. And it always *felt* our schemes had a chance.

I looked over at my bedside table, at the framed photo of Mom, Dad, Ryan, and me from my lower school graduation: Mom, Dad, and me all looking straight at the camera, and Ryan looking down and to the side but smiling his real smile.

I wasn't sure who I missed more—Ryan or the old version

of me who believed I could make anything happen, at least when I was at Audrey's quiet, orderly house. Our house is just as calm as hers now, but I'd given up on my big idea in less than twenty-four hours.

Please??? she added, and I snapped my new laptop shut. I needed a break anyway.

Sounds good. Leaving now, I wrote back, and she replied right away with five smiley faces and two hearts.

The Starbucks in C Hill, she added.

It made me a little sad that she thought she had to say that. Yeah, things have been kind of off lately, and we haven't gone there for a while, but it's the only one within walking distance. Right on the Ave., across from . . .

I stopped.

Maybe the laptop thing was a no-go, but that wasn't the only way I could do something good.

Mom had already nagged me until I wore the shirts and sweater she got me, but the jeans still sat inside crisp white tissue paper in the bag, with their $139 price tag attached.

I grabbed the bag, yelled a quick goodbye to Mom and Dad, and waved to Carl and Anne as I passed their yard. I could meet the new girl later.

I walked as fast as I could, but when I peeked into the Starbucks, I spotted Audrey from behind, already in line with her straight black hair in a ponytail.

This would only take a minute, though. It was important.

I crossed the street and opened the door to the consignment shop. Aunt Jill had taken me there once, and she'd picked out new black pants for work and a dress to wear to a wedding.

"Best store I've ever been to," she told me. "You get all the last-season gems these Chestnut Hill ladies get rid of to make room for their brand-new wardrobes."

There wasn't anybody at the counter, so I stood there at the front, guessing how much they'd give me for the jeans and picturing the look on Jenna's face when I went to the OT center to deliver an envelope stuffed full of cash.

I remembered one time when she was at our house last year, a few days before Audrey's family's annual Christmas party. Mrs. Lee had asked Ryan if he wanted to play some Christmas carols on the piano during the party, and Ry had said yes, but I could tell he was nervous about it. Sometimes Jenna helped Ryan get ready for overwhelming stuff by making lists and schedules ahead of time, so he'd know exactly what was coming. So I asked if they wanted me to write up a list of everyone I knew who would be at the party and the schedule of what usually happened in what order, since Ryan and Dad hadn't stayed very long the last couple of years.

Jenna gave me a huge smile. "What a thoughtful suggestion, Lauren. You're such a helpful sister."

I can't be "such a helpful sister" anymore, when Ryan's not even here. But now I can help other people instead.

I was so busy wondering whether I should tell Jenna to use the money for Hailey with the puffy ponytail or to choose who needed it most that I didn't notice when a woman in a black dress crossed the store and stepped behind the register.

She gave me a smile that lasted a millisecond. "How can I help you?"

"Uh, I want to sell these." I put the jeans on the counter between us. "Please."

She unfolded them and made an "mmm" noise as she examined the front and then the back.

"They've never even been tried on," I added, in case that was a selling point.

"Do you have a receipt for these by any chance?" she asked as she put them back down on the counter.

I didn't like the way she was looking at me, with her lips squeezed together as if she'd just downed a cup of the fresh-squeezed lemonade Audrey and I tried to sell the summer before third grade, before her mom told us you had to add sugar.

"Why?" I asked.

Then she raised her unnaturally skinny eyebrows, and I got it. She thought the jeans were stolen.

I dug into the bag, and luckily Mom's receipt was there, clinging to the top layer of tissue paper. I thrust it at the sour-faced lady, but she didn't tell me sorry for getting the wrong idea.

"They're great jeans," she said, looking me up and down. "And they look like your size. You sure you don't want them?"

"Positive."

She held up both her hands, as if she'd done everything she could to talk sense into me.

"All right, then." She opened a drawer and pulled out a sheet of paper. "Here's a form for you to fill out. You'll get forty percent of the profit if we're able to sell them."

At first I thought I'd heard her wrong.

"Forty percent?" I said. *"If?"*

"We're a consignment store," she said, enunciating every syllable. "That means you only get your commission if your item sells. That's how we stay in business, and that's how we're able to sell such beautiful things."

My phone buzzed. Probably Audrey, getting impatient.

"Well, how long do you think it'll take to sell the jeans?" I asked. "And how much would you sell them for?"

She gave me that millisecond-long, fake smile again. "We'd probably price the jeans at eighty dollars, but there's no way to know for sure whether they'll sell. You get the item back if it doesn't sell in sixty days."

Another customer wanted to look at a necklace inside a locked case, so she left me there at the front of the store.

Forty percent of $80 . . . $32 for $139 jeans, *if* somebody wanted them?

My phone buzzed again, and another employee, who'd been hanging up clothes, walked over and cleared her throat. At first I thought she was going to get mad at me for having my phone on, like at school.

"You could try online," she said quietly. "You can get closer to what those are worth that way, if you need the cash."

I started to tell her it wasn't like that—I didn't need the cash, exactly. But *other* people did, so what difference did it make?

I thanked her and stuffed the jeans back into the bag. And as I crossed the street back to Starbucks, I tried to plan my next steps. If I sold the jeans online, what site would I use? Would I send them in the regular mail? How would someone pay me? And what else did I have that I could sell?

Inside, Audrey was sitting at one of the front tables with a half-melted Frappuccino for each of us.

"Finally!" she said as I slid into the chair across from her. "What happened to you? I have a flute lesson this afternoon. I barely have any time to hang out now."

"I'm really sorry." I didn't want to tell her why I'd made her wait, so I just said, "Family stuff."

Her face softened immediately, as if she'd just done the expression-switch we used to do when we were little kids. Hold up a hand in front of our foreheads. Slide it down and frown. Slide back up and smile.

But she didn't ask what was going on or if it had to do with Ryan. Why would she, when she just assumes everything is so wonderful at Piedmont? Every once in a while, she says something like, "Aw, this song reminds me of Ry!" or, "Tell Ryan hi for me!" but that's it. It's like she thinks, OK, we talked about Ryan leaving for five minutes back at the end of August, so that conversation topic is taken care of, and now we can just move on.

"Well, you're here now," she said. "I have a scheme to discuss!"

She paused to examine my face, probably making sure I wasn't too upset about the fake family drama she didn't really want to talk about. I tried to look normal as I took a long, cold sip of my drink.

"Three words," she said once she was satisfied that I was OK. "Field. Hockey. Captains! What do you think?"

"Um, for next year, you mean?"

"Yes! We could start practicing together outside of school, like we did in third grade when we wanted to be the best at that Presidential Fitness thing."

I didn't remind her about how our Presidential Fitness Test training plan had turned out: Our stomach muscles were so sore from all our sit-ups practice that we both tanked on the actual test.

"We could run together to get faster, and we could work on passing and dribbling and stuff. There are even sleepaway field-hockey camps we could go to next summer!"

"That sounds fun," I said.

But it didn't, really. I like field hockey. I like how my mind goes blank while we run at the beginning of practice, and I like the rush of sprinting up the field and yelling for the ball when I'm near the net. I like the cracking sound it makes when I take a big swing and connect just right, and I like that I'm one of only three seventh graders who start on the A team. But that doesn't mean I want to spend all my time trying to become a field hockey star. It's just . . . who cares?

"I was thinking I could offer to switch to fullback, since Grace got hurt," Audrey added. "Then I'd probably get more playing time, and I could practice defending you, so we'd both get better."

"Sure," I said.

She took out her phone to type notes for the scheme and yanked off her thick silver cuff bracelet because it kept sliding up and down her arm.

The bracelet sat there on the table, next to Audrey's drink, glimmering in the sun that streamed through the window.

Maybe I could sell jewelry online, too. People might buy bracelets or necklaces or whatever more often than jeans, since you don't have to try on jewelry.

"I feel like you're not adding any ideas. Are you not into this?" Audrey asked.

"It's not that. You've just thought of so much good stuff!" I said, and she bought it.

She used to always know when I was faking something.

Maybe I've had too much practice at it lately and gotten too good. She barely even flinched last weekend when she invited me to go shopping and I told her Mom was making me stay home to clean my room.

A few minutes later, her dad texted to say he was outside, and she jumped up to meet him. "Do you want a ride?"

"It's fine," I told her. "It's nice out. I'll walk."

She slurped up the end of her drink and hurried out the door, leaving the silver bracelet there on the table.

She probably won't even notice she lost it—that's how much jewelry Audrey has. I picked it up so I could give it back later, and it was heavier than it looked. Real silver, probably.

I slid it into my bag, wondering how much somebody might pay for it if I didn't have to give it back. And how much somebody would give me for the jeans, once I figured out how to sell them online. A lot, probably. Enough to do something way more important than figuring out how to be captain of the field hockey team in eighth grade.

I started to head back home, and a few blocks in, I saw a flash of blond hair, bouncing, and then Anne and Carl's sweet, stringy gray dog, Seeger. The girl from the window.

"Hey!" I called. "Wait up!"

SIERRA

Expressions

Carl says one of their values as a family
is to respect and revere nature.
And that they expect their foster children to follow suit.

They show me:
the compost,
the garden,
the "rainwater reclamation system."
"Working the land is good for the spirit," Carl tells me.

Does he have a *Chicken Soup for the Soul* expression for
everything?

Mom's favorite
AA expression is
Fake it till you make it.
She used to say it even
drink in hand.
Maybe I can fake this

till Mom can get me back.
Not make more trouble.

Carl hands me a rake

I fake a smile, then start to pile the leaves.
      Red. Green. Brown.
Carl shows me his system. Raking onto a tarp.

But Seeger keeps jumping into the piles.
      System   broken.

      Carl winces. Anne laughs.

Another Unfamiliar Corner

After raking,
Carl asks me to take Seeger on a walk.
Anne says when I get back,
she'll pour us some sun tea.
I wonder if that's like the sweet, powdery kind
Cassidy and I would eat with our fingers sometimes.

Each house castlelike, old.
Seeger doesn't pull, lets me lead.
We walk around another unfamiliar corner.
The girl with the long brown hair from the window
runs toward me, bag in hand, smiling.
                    I want to run the other way
but remember some of Mom's advice over the years:

> *Don't let them know you're hurting, or they'll try to get you.*
> *Wear a smile, but protect your heart.*

She says her name's Lauren, asks if I just moved in.
I nod. Trying to grin.

Seeger wags his tail at her, licks her hand.
Her hair's in loose, movie-star waves. Pearls in her ears.
But she wears a sweatshirt, jeans with a hole in the knee.
Asks if she can walk with me, where I'm going to school,
how old I am.
Same school, Northwest Friends School,
same grade, seventh.
Same bus stop.
She almost squeals, says she'll pick me up Monday morning.

We can walk

together.

I grin, shrug,
run a hand through my hair,
as stringy as the dog's.

Blue Already

This new room, blue already,
reminds me of when Mom
would stash me at Nan's so she could party all night.
      Sometimes she would leave me for weeks. A month
         once.

Nan's pull-out in the den, hard like this bed.
The blanket here isn't a comforter,
it's an old quilt, smells like Nan's basement.
      Nan with her yellow teeth and Jell-O.
      Nan who died from all that smoking.

I don't know what to wear to this new school tomorrow.
Wish I had asked Lauren.
I try to sleep
      but, instead,
      pretend I'm back in my first room ever
      back when things were better
      parents still together
      my Rapunzel posters,
      my Target-brand American Girl doll, Cynthia.

Instead of sleeping, I spin back in time,
dress Cynthia
for school.

The Morning

I throw on jeans and a sweatshirt.
Anne's gotten up with me,
says Carl's already at work,
at the co-op.
I look at her, confused.
She explains
the co-op is a food market,
Carl works as a manager.
I want to ask why
they don't call it a grocery store, but I don't.

Anne's wearing an oversized, sweater,
clunky jewelry, and big headband.
Think of Mom's Wawa uniform.
Her tanks and minis,
her small gold heart necklace.
Anne's gotten me cereal,
some kind of granola.
Missing my Corn Pops,
tell her I can do it myself.

She says, beaming, that she's happy to,
she's got lots of energy, she says,
she loves the morning.

I don't tell her, but I want to say, *I do, too.*
The morning is when good things happen.
Better than anything the night before.

Curiosity

On time, as promised,
Lauren's here.
>In a puffy red vest and sweater.
>With two chocolate muffins.

Anne told me this morning
Lauren has an autistic brother,
he's gone away, a special school.
Lauren takes my arm.
>My old jean jacket links with
>her soft white sweater.
>>Like we're friends already.

And though I know we aren't,
it does make this day
something less scary.

At the bus stop,
Lauren knows everyone.

But on the bus, she sits with me.
Wonder whether she used to sit
with her brother,
if they even went to the same school.
Wonder what's changed
since he left.

She asks me so many questions, like Anne,
                but she looks at me
                with real curiosity,
not like a grown-up trying to be nice.

Not sure what I can give this girl,
who, besides this missing brother,
seems to have everything.
Why does she need me?

                Shiny necklace on now, beads swinging.
                Shiny bright teeth, like she already had braces.

But she laughs when I ask—
the bus wheezing onto the curb—
whether a Friends school means
they make you be nice to everybody?

Chain of Hearts

This school's old, too.
Not like my old junior high,
it had white walls and red lockers.
These walls, painted with murals,
no lockers, you share a "space,"
      which is really a cubby, like in elementary.
How come a school costs so much money
when it's old and you have to share?

Lauren's in my advisory.
She has an Asian friend, Audrey,
hair black, straight to her shoulders.
I can tell they've been friends a long time,
their inside jokes light the room.
I watch the way other people watch them.
But mid-laugh,
      Lauren seems to remember something.

She walks away from Audrey,
            to me.
As she walks, I doodle Mom's signature doodle:
      a line of hearts chained to other hearts
        one heart up, one down, up, down, never-ending,
I line the whole page,
pretending I wasn't
      one of the others, all of us
          watching.

Joining

I tell Lauren she doesn't have to sit with me,
  but she says she wants to,
   says she just joined a group.
     She looks at Audrey quickly
     Audrey looks at her then away.
Says it's called
  Worship & Ministry
  (sounds like something out of Nan's church).
Thinks it might be just what I need.
Wonder how she thinks she knows so much
   already about me.

I miss Cassidy, us laughing together
watching TV or bowling.
Our moms letting us stay at the arcade
for hours.
Finding quarters on the floor.
Or at school, partners in gym.
Studying for tests.
I look at Audrey, what's there to lose, I agree.

Tricks or Treats

Our homeroom (they call it advisory)
is run by Ms. Meadows.
She makes an announcement about Halloween,
     says Quakers:
          don't wear costumes with weapons,
          don't wear costumes that appropriate other cultures.
Not sure what she means by this
maybe, like, when I was seven
and Mom went as Pocahontas?
          Her long wig covering her hair like mine.
          I hid her wig,
          didn't want her to cover up our matching hair.
Wonder if these seventh graders
     even still wear costumes anymore.
          Before they took me from Mom,
          before that terrible last day at the mall,
          before Mom's lucky streak of green days ran out,
Cassidy and I had plans to trick-or-treat.
Mom said we were too old for that crap,
I told her no one's too old for chocolate.
She said,   *No matter what the day, my Sierra girl,*
                    green, orange, you always make me laugh.

The Weight Between Us

After school,
Anne's home,
says she will be here, *every day*, for me.

Is that supposed to be comforting?
I do one of those fake smiles.

She asks how school was
she wants to know everything
about my day.
Or anything I'm willing to share.
She says all this while stringing beads on wire.

    I tell her it was fine, Lauren's nice.
             Give her a little so she doesn't ask more.
    I don't tell her how the worry I feel for Mom
                feels like wearing a life jacket made of lead.
I don't tell her that without Mom
I feel like I'm
         sinking.

She pauses, puts down her project, looks me in the eye,
tells me her mother was an alcoholic.
That she grew up living with her grandmother.

I know she is saying this to try to
lighten the weight between us.

But looking out the window,
                    trees shedding leaves,
the only way I can imagine
    feeling calm again
            is by being with Mom,
            any room, any apartment,
            it doesn't matter.
I need to be there
to make sure she is sober.
Don't they know
I am the only one who can do any of that for her?

They say now I am safe—but I'm not the one in danger.
                    With me here
who's going to take care of   her?

Gnaws & Wishes

The feeling gnaws at me.
I need to know how she is.
Our call's not scheduled for a few days.
I text Cassidy:

> *Has my mom called yours?*

Cassidy:

> *Dunno. Mom's out.*
> *That annoying Brian again.*
> *School sucked 2day.*
> *Come back!!*

I curl up into my blue room
and wish, wish, wish I could.

LAUREN

Costumes for Three

The day I met Sierra, I listed the jeans online for $100. And by the time I got home from school on Sierra's first day, somebody had already sent me the money on PayPal.

It wasn't even that hard to mail them. I told Mom I was working on a history project with Audrey after field hockey practice yesterday, and I got off at Audrey's bus stop instead of mine. I told Audrey that was because Mom needed me to do an errand, and then I just walked to the post office to package up the jeans. Then I went to the bank to take the $100 out of the account Dad opened for me last spring, when I started earning babysitting money, because I know he can check the account balance online. Easy as anything. No problem at all.

And I finally got a video message back from Ryan yesterday, too. He showed me the three guppies in his tiny tank—one red, one green, one blue—and told me about his new friend Ellie, who knows just as much about Ancient Egypt as he does and thinks his fish are awesome. He said Scott the OT might take them to an aquarium that's half an hour away the next time they have a free weekend day. But I looked up the aquarium on my phone, and it doesn't have hippos like the one in Camden does. And the shark tank doesn't look anywhere near as good, and it might be crowded if Scott hasn't been before and doesn't know the right time to go. Or what if Ellie doesn't *actually* like fish as much as Ryan does and she doesn't have fun at the aquarium, and Ry thinks the whole day is going to be great, but then it's just a giant disappointment?

At the end of his message, Ry asked me to make my next video in front of his fish tank, so he could see how his other fish are doing.

So I took the $100 down to the basement and fed the fish a quarter of a teaspoon of flake food, just the way Ry taught me before he left. When all the fish came out to eat, I made sure I got every single one on my video, even the two little Cory catfish that like to hide behind plants. At least this way he can watch all his fish and know that I'm taking good care of them, even if the aquarium trip isn't what he's expecting.

Then after I sent the message, I stashed the $100 at the bottom of a tub of old puzzles in the storage part of the basement, and I put Audrey's silver bracelet there, too. I'll give it back if she mentions it, definitely. I'll probably even give it back if she doesn't. But she was wearing a different one today—a thick chain with a heart dangling off it, from Tiffany's. And I just . . . I don't know. I sort of can't deal with Audrey right now.

In advisory this morning, Ms. Meadows went over the same old Halloween costume rules we have to listen to every year. Then Audrey, Sierra, and I went to the space outside the classroom to get our stuff for first period.

"How about we dress up as salt and pepper shakers this

year?" Audrey said. "Ooh, or ketchup and mustard? Angel and devil? Elphaba and Glinda?"

I looked at Sierra, who was *right there*, paging through a notebook, and tried to send Audrey a message with my eyes.

"Lauren! Halloween's next week! We're running out of time." Audrey snapped her fingers. Completely clueless.

Is it really that hard for Audrey to see how sad Sierra looks when she lets herself take a break from smiling for two seconds? Does Audrey just not pay attention to *anything* that doesn't have to do with her? I still don't know what happened that means Sierra has to live with Anne and Carl instead of her own mom and dad. But it was a big deal, obviously, whatever it was. Sierra could use some friends.

Not that she's my charity case or anything. She's funny, and she's just . . . different. She asks questions about stuff I've never stopped to think about, like why we don't have real lockers at school, except for gym, and why there's so much stone in our neighborhood. Stone houses, stone walls, stone slabs along the sidewalks. I'd never really noticed until she pointed it out.

And she wears Target brand shoes instead of Vans or Converse or lace-up boots like everybody else, and she's never met Ryan. So when I told her about him going away to school, she didn't say, "Well, he said he wanted to go, Lauren. And the website looks so nice!" the way Audrey did. She just said, "North Carolina's far. You must really miss your brother." So then I told her about Family Weekend and how Piedmont's supposedly so great but I just know it's wrong for Ryan and there's nothing I can do about it.

Not wrong the way the Keller School was. Piedmont's not wrong for everybody who goes there, probably. Maybe it's a great place for Ryan's new friend Ellie. But wrong for Ryan, because he should be home with us and his fish tank and his favorite Philadelphia places and his routines.

And Sierra nodded like she really understood, and then she said, "If you ever want to talk about him more, you can." And I wanted to hug her, but I didn't want to spook her again.

As Audrey stood there, tapping the toe of her boot on the ground and waiting for me to respond about Halloween, I grabbed my Spanish stuff and found a pencil that still had lead. Then I took a step back, so I was even with Sierra. "How about Charlie's Angels? All three of us could do it. Remember we saw that movie once, Aud? With your parents?"

Audrey nodded, but her face had gone all pinched, just like it had the other day when she asked if I wanted to go for an extra field-hockey training run after school, since we didn't have practice, but I'd already promised Sierra we'd take the bus home together.

"With Lucy Liu and the two white actresses," Audrey said. "I remember."

"So what do you think?"

She stuck her chin out. "Lucy Liu is Chinese, Lauren. Not Korean."

Oops. "Well, I think the actresses in the original version were all white. I . . . I don't know if their race is really that important."

Audrey's chin only jutted out farther, and I didn't really blame her. That hadn't come out right at all.

"Hey, how about the three little pigs, then? That could be kind of cute." Or it would have been when we were five, anyway, but I couldn't think of anything else. "What do you think, Sierra?"

Sierra was hugging her notebook to her chest now, and her mouth curled into a small smile. "Are you sure that's not a-whatever-ating the pig culture?"

I burst out laughing, and Sierra's smile got bigger. A lot of the time it doesn't seem real, the way Sierra smiles, but this smile was. I could tell.

"Good point. If we're sure it isn't appropriating the pig culture, what do you think of going as the three little pigs, Aud?"

Audrey's mouth was still all pinched up, and now she wrinkled her nose, too. "Two of the three little pigs die, you know."

Mr. Ellis peeked out into the hallway and told us all to hurry up and get to class.

"My mom bought this really beautiful beaded mask for a masquerade ball benefit thing. Maybe I'll just wear that," Audrey said. Then she took off for science without saying goodbye.

Sierra's brown eyes were extra big when she watched Audrey go. "What version of 'The Three Little Pigs' did *she* read?"

I laughed again as I linked my arm through Sierra's, and we went down the hall together to Spanish.

At lunchtime, Sierra was coming with me to Worship and Ministry.

"It's technically supposed to be one person per advisory," I explained as we went down to the cafeteria to get our food. "But Mr. Ellis said it's fine for you to come, since so many advisories don't have representatives."

Audrey was already sitting at our usual table, with Emma

and a couple of other friends. I started to wave to her as Sierra and I walked by, but she looked away.

I remembered when Aunt Jill picked me up after Audrey's fifth-grade birthday party. "Audrey is used to getting her way, huh?" she said to Mom when she dropped me off at home.

Aunt Jill was right, obviously. And now I'm finding out what happens when I don't cooperate.

Sierra and I took our lunches upstairs, and only Mr. Ellis and Mariah were already there in his classroom. I took the chair next to Mariah, and Sierra took the one next to me.

"I'm so glad you're joining us, Sierra!" Mr. Ellis said when we came in. "Great to see you, girls."

And the thing about Mr. Ellis is, it always feels like he really *does* think it's great to see us.

Jake showed up next, wearing an orangey-red shirt. The last time I went shopping with Audrey, before camp, I tried on a bathing suit that was almost that same exact shade, and she shook her head. "I don't think that's your color. But don't feel bad. Orange doesn't look good on anybody."

She was wrong, though, because it looked good on Jake, with his light brown skin. Really good. I've seen Jake's parents at school stuff, and his dad is black and his mom is white—the opposite of Anne and Carl next door. I never got to meet Anne and Carl's daughter, Amy, but I imagine her with skin the same color as Jake's.

He caught me looking at him, so I focused my eyes on my tray and stuffed half a chicken finger into my mouth. Then Gordy came in with another sixth grader he'd recruited to join—a kid named Oscar—and Mr. Ellis got us started talking about our simplicity initiative.

"Mariah, Jake, I hear you were a huge part of planning the recycling initiative last year," Mr. Ellis said. "What awesome ideas are you sitting on now?"

Jake shrugged, and Mariah smoothed down her blue bangs.

"Stewardship was easier than simplicity," Jake said. "We just had to think of what we could do to help the environment. We found out lots of people threw away stuff that's recyclable, so we made signs to hang in the cafeteria and the halls about what you can recycle and what you can't."

I remembered them standing up during morning meeting to announce the recycling signs: Mariah fidgeting with her hair, which was still dirty blond then, and Jake standing up tall, enunciating as if he'd practiced at home.

Mr. Ellis nodded. "Well, that might not have been hard to do, but it made a big impact. Often the best ideas are the *simplest* ones. No pun intended."

"We also gave a prize to the advisory that filled up a recycling bin the fastest," Mariah reminded Jake. "Everybody likes prizes."

"Maybe we'll offer some kind of prize this year, too," Mr. Ellis said. He wrote the word *prize* on the board with a question mark.

Mariah nodded. "It's harder to come up with an initiative for simplicity than stewardship, though."

Mr. Ellis sat back down. "Well, let's go ahead and get our brainstorm on! *Hard* doesn't mean *impossible*. I have faith."

Jake took out a notebook and started scribbling a brainstorming web, with the word *simplicity* in the middle. He crossed something out, frowning down at the page.

Meanwhile, Mariah, Gordy, and Gordy's friend Oscar

pretended to be fascinated by their lunches, and Sierra stared out the window, watching leaves spin in the breeze.

Sierra understands simplicity better than any of us. She doesn't wear brand-name clothes. She didn't have a phone until Carl gave her his old one, and it doesn't even get Internet. I thought she'd feel comfortable in this group. I thought she could . . . I don't know. Lead us in the right direction. Guide us. But maybe that was just as wrong as when I told Audrey it doesn't matter what race Charlie's Angels are.

At the front of the room, Mr. Ellis was looking at me as if he was counting on me and my "strong sense of social responsibility" to get us going. But I had nothing.

There was a red flyer hanging on the bulletin board behind Mr. Ellis's head. *Join us for the Philadelphia AIDS Walk this weekend!*

A walk. Mom, Dad, Ry, and I all did an Autism Acceptance Walk last April. I joined a fund-raising team and got people to sponsor me.

"We could have a Simplicity-a-Thon!"

I said it so loudly, Sierra jumped in her seat.

"A Simplicity-a-Thon?" Jake echoed, but his voice was interested, not sarcastic.

"It would be a whole day when people can't use any electronics or buy anything. Anybody who wants to participate could get people to sponsor them by making a donation. And we'd give the money to a really good cause. To people who actually need it."

"And we could give a prize for whoever raises the most!" Mariah added.

Mr. Ellis wrote it on the board: *Simplicity-a-Thon*. Then he added an exclamation point and underlined it twice.

And once the idea seal was broken, I got another one. "We could have a Simplicity Prize on Halloween, too! For the best homemade costume!"

"We could make signs this week, maybe," Mariah said. "To try to get people to make their own costumes instead of buying them."

Mr. Ellis wrote down the Halloween idea, and then Sierra spoke up.

"Um . . . I think I have an idea."

Everybody turned to her, and she shrank down smaller in her chair, but she said it anyway.

"Maybe around the holidays, we could encourage people to do favors for other people instead of buying them stuff? It's something my mom and I used to do when . . ." She paused for a second before she finished the thought. "Some years."

Mr. Ellis smiled at her. "A Favor Swap. What an awesome idea!"

And it was. So much better than the Secret Gifter Swaps we usually did in advisory, when everybody wasted ten bucks on candy or iTunes gift cards for whichever person they got assigned. I *knew* it had been the right thing to get Sierra to come to the group.

On the way out, Jake stopped us. "Good job today. I'm glad you both joined."

My cheeks went warm. "Thanks."

"See ya!" He took one hand off his lunch tray to give us a little wave, and we watched him go. But he said hi to three different people in the hallway before he made it even five feet from the classroom, so it probably wasn't that special that he'd stopped to talk to us.

"Are *you* glad you joined?" I asked Sierra.

"I liked it, yeah," she said. Then she leaned in close to whisper. "Will Audrey be mad about the Simplicity Prize at Halloween if she wears that mask, though?"

I thought of Audrey's pinched-up face that morning and the way she'd looked away from me in the cafeteria. She would definitely be mad if she knew I'd come up with a prize she wouldn't have a shot at winning. A little voice inside me said, "So let her be!"

But this was Audrey, who had spent an entire afternoon building a guinea-pig obstacle course with me. Whose house I'd had double sleepovers at on weekends sometimes and whose family always took me to the Poconos for New Year's. Who used to get Ryan to show her his fish tank when she came over and then ask what the different breeds and plants were called.

"I'll talk to her," I promised. "She'll change her mind about the costume. We'll do one for three people, all of us."

But Sierra didn't look convinced.

That night, Dad came home for dinner and picked up pizza on the way. Even though we weren't eating anything special, Mom set the dining room table with fancy silverware, fancy plates, and matching placemats and cloth napkins. She put fresh flowers in the middle—orange, red, and yellow ones—in a brand-new vase the same shade of yellow as the smallest flowers.

She said she'd bought it because she "needed a cheerful

little pick-me-up," and Dad complimented her on how pretty everything looked.

But I was thinking about how Aunt Jill once told me that she and Mom hadn't gotten along that well when they were younger. Mom was so orderly. So focused on keeping everything neat and matching and perfect, and Aunt Jill was "wild," whatever that meant. She said Mom had let go of some of that need for things to look just right. Thanks to Ryan, Mom's priorities had changed, and they understood each other better now.

But now maybe Mom is turning back into the version of herself that Aunt Jill didn't get along with. That I never even met at all.

"I got tickets to the Eagles game this weekend," Dad said when we all sat down.

For a second, I got excited. We used to have Dad-and-Lauren days, when Mom would do something else with Ry. Dad's a Philly sports nut, and Mom and Ry don't really like going to games, but I do. I could always tell how happy it made Dad that I knew the players' names and who was having a good year and who wasn't. And it made me happy, too, to have something that was just for the two of us.

"Upper level?" I asked.

Those are the seats he used to get, way up high. He'd pick me up and hold me over his shoulders when the Eagles scored a touchdown, and I felt like I was flying.

"Even better," he said. "Box seats from the firm. For all three of us!"

Then he started explaining the gourmet food we'd have to choose from, and how we wouldn't be cold even if it was chilly because we could stay inside, and how there were brand-new

TVs in every box. Which somehow people think they need even though they are literally in the place where the game is being played?

"You know I'm not wild about football," Mom said. "But even I think that sounds fun!"

But *I* thought it sounded terrible. The whole Dad-and-Lauren upper-level experience ruined so we could go to a fancy party that happened to be at a game.

"I don't think I can go this weekend," I said. "It's almost Halloween. I have to make my costume with Audrey and Sierra."

Dad's face fell.

"We can buy you a costume, sweetie," Mom said.

I stood up. "No! I need to make it!"

They both stared at me as if they weren't so sure who I was anymore, but *they're* the ones who keep changing. Not me.

I excused myself to work on homework, but instead I went back to the site where I'd posted the jeans.

I almost posted Audrey's bracelet, but then I got this picture in my mind of her crouched down next to me on her driveway, grinning as she set up the last block for our guinea-pig maze, and I couldn't.

So instead I posted the signed Brian Dawkins jersey Dad gave me a few Christmases ago. People pay a ton for jerseys, especially if they're signed, and everyone loves Brian Dawkins. Dad got the jersey signed for me at some fund-raiser he went to right after the Eagles had a special ceremony to retire Dawkins's number, because he was that good. I'm sure somebody will pay a lot for it.

And if Dad only wants to watch games from a suite, then there's no reason I'll need to wear it again.

SIERRA

FATES

Audrey invited Lauren and me
over to make our costumes.
I was pretty sure she only invited Lauren,
me, tagging along
like when I was 8
     and Mom and I lived with Nan.
Because we had no other choice.
     She and Dad still shared custody,
          he wasn't dealing yet.
          He would bring me to Uncle Al's
          with Tammy or his buddies,
          I would sit on a bar stool, drink Cokes, play
               solitaire,
          and he would call me his *smart kid*, mumbling
               into his whiskey.

Audrey's house has a huge front room,
on a huge wooden table
fabric
markers
thread
in neat lines.

Audrey asks if her housekeeper can get us a snack before we
    get to work.
Lauren asks for Coke & chips,
but when I say no thanks,
she says forget it,

"I don't need anything, either."

Says it like she's got something to prove.
Audrey glares, my heart pounds.

Doesn't Lauren know what she's doing?
        Tempting the Fates.

                That's what Tammy would say about Dad.
                Another drink, man, and you tempt the Fates.
                He would say, he was *a tempting sort of man.*

"So what should we do that would work for three? But also
    embody simplicity?"
Lauren asks. Ignoring Audrey's glare.
                My mind still on tooth-stained Tammy, Dad.
"The three Fates?" I suggest.

"Like in that movie *Hercules* we loved in, like, second grade.
There's the spinner, the one who measures,
and then the one who cuts.
Remember, Audrey?"
Lauren asks. Audrey's stare fades, she giggles.

My heart pounds slow down.
We work, with
scissors,
string,
tape.

Maybe me coming here,
                    Tammy's slurring words
                        echoing in my head
                            spin,
                            measure,
                            cut,
wasn't by mistake?

But, Then

Audrey   says
she   doesn't   want   to be
the   one   with the scissors
the   crone   who designates death
she   wants   to be the spinner
Lauren   says
Sierra's   perfect   for the young blond spinner
Audrey   looks   like   she   might cry
I   tell them   I don't care   what Fate I am.

But it's too late
we   split   in bits   like all   this string
                   scattered on   the polished floor.

So Many Things

On the way home,
Lauren tells me to ignore Audrey,
that she's always been too possessive.
She needs to get over it.

Lauren tells me we can do our own costumes.

> Without her.

My stomach lurches.
>How can I take away Lauren's anger?
>Make things the way they were before?
I think how when our moms would get wasted together,
Cassidy and I would pretend her room
was the mall.
Dress her younger sisters in scarves and old high heels.
Pretend her broken toys and DVD cases with no movies
were things worth buying.

How we distracted ourselves from our moms singing
too loud, falling down, inviting over men.

I ask her if she wants to keep working
at her house.

Lauren asks if we can go to my house instead.
At first I don't know what she means.

I don't have a house.

But I nod
when she says at Anne's there's more
inspiration for simplicity.
"No kidding," I say.
She laughs.
Anne tries to give us raisins and carrots
on the way to my room,
but Lauren follows me now when I say no.
I make a funny face on the way up,
trying to make her laugh again.
Remind myself of Cassidy, always joking
away discomfort.

I trace a line of dust across the floor
as she starts to brainstorm simple things:
A candle,
vegetables,
the sea.

> Flash to my mother
> a beach in Wildwood,
> a towel, her curled in next to me.
> We play the cloud game,
> she takes swigs from a flask,
> but I don't care, 'cause she's safe with me.

I see a dragon.
She sees her favorite flower.

"I could be a sunflower,"
I say to Lauren.
She nods, beaming.
Look at my kaleidoscope,
think of the color for friendship.
"You could be something else yellow."

"Yes!" she says, almost jumping up from the wooden chair.
Seeger comes in then, licking her hand, she laughs.
He knocks a pencil off the wooden desk.

She picks it up.
Beaming again.
She knows just what she's going to be.

I know I've done it.
Taken away Audrey's angry words
and made her
sun-stream
happy.

Containing

Sunday,
Lauren texts me a yellow heart
says she's so excited about our costumes.
On the way to grocery shopping with Anne,
I text her, too, a smiley face.
We get to the co-op,
tiny compared to the Giant grocery store.
Bumpy, lumpy fruit and veggies.
You put your food in big gray bins, not carts.

Anne knows everyone.
Doesn't introduce me as a foster kid, just:
"This is Sierra, she's new to the neighborhood."

I look down, manage some hellos.

"Go up those stairs . . . to the bulk section.
There's candy . . ." she says, smiling.

Is she bribing me?
Thinks if I get candy, I'll talk more?
But I go,
my mouth drops at all the bins.
Container after container of
noodles,
beans,
flour.

36 types of granola.
Is this supposed to be simple, too?

There's even candy in bulk.
Jelly beans, chocolates.
I wonder why
they don't just sell
Skittles or M&M's in packages.

Shrug to myself, fill a bag up.

And when I go back down, Anne says peach rings, her
     favorite.

"Yeah, they're okay, I guess,"
I say but don't offer her any.
Keep the sugar tart taste all to myself.

In–Between

When we get home, lugging groceries,
candy in hand,
I know what's coming.
Each Sunday,
I'm supposed to have a
"feelings-level conversation"
with Anne and Carl,
according to Maude.
I try to answer their questions
with yes and no,
information that will not lead
to more questions:
  "Yes, I am making friends."
  "No, I don't miss my parents too much."
I chew peach rings in between.
Rub sugar dust,
finger
to
finger.

To Rest

Carl says he needs help
with garden chores.
He says he's putting the garden
to rest for the winter.
He has me pull out all the basil;
he says Anne makes the best pesto.
I don't tell him I don't know what that is.
The smell of the basil reminds me
of Dad.
He told me once fresh basil
made everything better.
His Italian grandmother told him so.
When Carl's not looking,
I put a leaf into my mouth.
Nibble it.

Carl doesn't make me talk,
but he does make me work hard.
After we're done, pulling plants
from each square,
laying down straw,
I ask him:
"Why do you like to do so much work?
Just for food?"

He laughs loudly,
I didn't think I was joking.

"Doesn't it feel good?
To take care of this land?"

I nibble a bit more on the basil leaf.
         Dad cracking open a beer as he put basil into sauce.
         Picking me up to stir it.
I shrug at Carl since
pretty sure all I feel

is tired.

Close By

Each Sunday evening,
both my parents call me.
Dad, always right at 6.
Always says the same things: food sucks, TV's not bad.
Asks me what I'm studying.
Says in prison he's gotten a hunger for learning.
I tell him about the garden. The basil.
He explains what pesto is.
Mom's time is not set. So I need to stay close by.
She has my new cell and their landline.
     I wait between phones.
Stomach growing fluttery with each minute she doesn't call,
like how I felt at Audrey's.
Except then,
there might've been something
I could've said to make them stop fighting.
Change fate,
switch colors,
spin,
measure,
cut,
     but with Mom?
I can't do anything anymore.
Maybe she's having an angry, orange day
and she won't call at all.

She Insists

Anne serves her "famous veggie lasagna,"
which is full of zucchini and other vegetables
my own parents never insisted I eat.
I sort the noodles, cheese, sauce
from the green things,
put them to the side.
Carl says I need to eat my greens.
Smiles, points to his EAT MORE KALE T-shirt.
Anne says she suspects
I've been eating nothing
but junk for years.
                    She assumes. Insists.
Her bracelets jangling from her wrists.
She doesn't know my dad worked restaurants,
that he could really cook.
That he used to show me how.
She doesn't know
when I was really little
we were almost like a regular family.
I keep eating the
noodles,
cheese,
sauce.
Tell her I need to be done so I can be ready for Mom
when she calls.
Anne's dark eyes soften then.

I excuse myself, rinse my plate.

Hours later,
Anne insists
I go to bed
and not wait up.
She says 10:00 P.M. is late
for a school night.
I roll my eyes
tell her my parents let me stay up till 1:00 A.M.
watching TV, school or no school.
She says that's not good parenting,
that kids need boundaries.
          Who is she to tell me
          what is good, what isn't?
She has a secret room
filled with a little girl's stuff—

if she was such a good parent,
how did she lose her own child?

I don't want to ask that question.
Or know the answer.

I don't say anything, just tell her
you can't make me go to bed.
She says this one time she will let me stay up.
          "But this will not keep happening."
She leaves, and I watch the clock.

The green digits glow in the night.
I imagine Mom
in a swirl of her own green.

Lucky, happy, safe.

Too Much Quiet

Up till midnight, Mom never called.
I called Maude, who didn't answer.
I texted Cassidy. Lena, even. No one could help.
In the morning,
Anne said she got an e-mail from Maude,
we will know more soon.
All she knows at the moment
is there's another court date set
"to evaluate Mom's behavior."
Like she's a kid sent to the principal.

I ask her if I can stay home,
think of all the times Mom let me.
How she found excuses to keep me close.
Anne says no.

In school, I sit in something they call Meeting
everyone just doing nothing
but being

quiet.

Wonder if this is what it feels
like in jail
or whether it's so loud there
you wish for
                    quiet.
Like at the funhouse carnival,
        trapped in noise.
Never looking quite
        like yourself.

Audrey stands up, says,
"Sometimes people aren't who you thought they were."

Lauren looks at me and sticks her tongue out.
I smile at her
stick my tongue out, too,

but what I
want to say is

                    too much quiet

might make everything
grow bigger—
taller,
wider—
than it needs to be.

Missed

Check my phone between classes,
see a missed call
from Mom's jail.

If Anne had let me stay home from school,
I would have answered it!

Anger swells in me
I want to throw my phone against the wall,
instead I run to the bathroom,
pound the heavy door shut,
let out a silent scream.

Latching On

After school,
I try to push my feelings aside.
Knowing Lauren needs my help.

We make posters and flyers for the costume contest
and the Simplicity-a-Thon,
Lauren's big bubble letters
          round and full and shaded
                    mine slant and squirm.

How can she smile at me, draw bubble letters,
when her best friend's so angry?
Doesn't she want to do everything she can
to wash that anger away?

I pretend to be happy, too, for Lauren's sake.
Don't think about Audrey's glares,
               Mom's call,
               Anne's lost little girl.

Instead, I—

slow my breath, latch my laugh on to Lauren's. Try to forget.
Rest my eyes on her big, bold letters:

S   I   M   P   L   I   C   I   T   Y

LAUREN

Partners in Justice

On Halloween, we have to wear regular clothes to school, so we can have a "focused and productive morning." Then anybody who has a costume changes in the locker room after lunch, and we all go to the gym for the Halloween assembly.

Most people bring their costumes to lunch and leave them in bags under their chairs. But Sierra left her flower costume outside Ms. Meadows's room, so I went with her to get it.

The hallways were so empty, I could hear our voices echo, even though we weren't talking loudly. There weren't any teachers around because they were all still in the cafeteria, and the kids who hadn't brought costumes were outside for recess.

"You want to change in the bathroom up here?" I asked.

Sierra straightened the bottom of her UNCLE AL'S BAR & GRILL T-shirt, which is too big for her, but on purpose, I think. It makes her look smaller than usual, and younger.

"Are we allowed?" she asked.

We weren't allowed, technically. But the bathroom right in front of us was empty, and the locker room downstairs was going to be packed. And it's not like we were going to have a soap war or pull all the paper towels out of the dispenser and leave them on the floor or anything.

I shrugged. "Who cares?"

Before this year, *I* would have. I cared about following every single rule at school, even if I thought the rule was silly. I felt like Mom and Dad worried a lot about Ry, and I couldn't risk making them worry about me, too.

But yesterday, when Mom and Dad thought I was staying after field hockey to make more Worship and Ministry posters, I went back to the post office and the bank because the Brian Dawkins jersey sold, too. Another $200, and nobody has any idea.

Last time Aunt Jill was over with my little cousin Melody, who's two and cries all the time, she joked to Mom that being around me had spoiled her because I always did what I was supposed to and almost never got upset when I didn't get what I wanted. My face burned as I thought of the times I *did* get upset about not getting my way: when Mom couldn't buy me new clothes for last year's spring dance, when only Audrey's mom was there to see me hit a home run at a softball game, when I said I was sick of going to the aquarium right before I went to camp and stayed home by myself instead. But Mom didn't correct Aunt Jill or anything. She just smiled.

And she laughed when Aunt Jill added, "You'd better hope Lauren's not in for a case of the very delayed Terrible Twos! The Terrible Twelves, maybe."

I know Aunt Jill was just kidding, but . . . I don't know. Maybe it's my turn to break some rules.

Sierra followed me into the empty bathroom. Audrey and

I are used to changing in front of each other, but Sierra went into one stall, so I went into another.

When we came out—Sierra in my green jeans and a green shirt, me in Ryan's old yellow T-shirt over leggings—we grinned at each other in the mirror. She helped me pin on my Crayola sign and adjust my pointy yellow hat, and I helped her straighten her sunflower headpiece.

Then we ran down the stairs into the gym and found seats. We're supposed to sit with our advisories at assemblies, but everything was too chaotic, and we ended up with Mr. Ellis's group instead. The sixth graders in costumes paraded past first, one at a time, except for the kids with group costumes, who all went together. Mr. Ellis, Ms. Meadows, and my sixth-grade math teacher, Mr. Warren, were the three judges, and they sat front and center, taking notes on clipboards.

A group of sixth-grade girls were dressed as characters from *Alice in Wonderland*, and that made me think of last year, when Audrey and I had organized that *Wizard of Oz* group. I looked for Audrey in the crowd, to see who she was sitting with and what she was wearing with her mom's beaded mask, but I couldn't find her.

The last sixth grader who paraded by was dressed as an iPhone. He'd made the costume on black poster board, with little square widgets across the front that looked just like the real ones—messaging, weather, e-mail, iTunes, and a blank one in the middle for his face. We were all supposed to applaud the same amount for everybody so no one would feel bad, but people cheered extra loud for the iPhone kid, and all three judges were smiling as they took notes. An iPhone doesn't exactly say, "Let's live simply," though. I scanned the crowd for other homemade costumes but didn't spot many people with good ones, except Jake, who was a monster, with a big old sweater pulled up over his forehead and two Ping-Pong balls painted to look like googly eyes glued on. Would it look like favoritism if Mr. Ellis picked Jake or Sierra or me for the Simplicity Prize?

When it was time for seventh graders to go, Sierra and I ended up close to the front of the line, behind a devil and angel and in front of a bunch of boys who were just wearing their Eagles and Flyers and 76ers gear. I walked by the judges with Sierra right after me. People clapped for us but nowhere near as loudly as they had for the iPhone kid. Then, just as we'd looped around and were looking for a place to sit back down, the crowd went wild.

"Looking good, Max!" an eighth grader yelled.

"Yeah, Audrey!"

Audrey?

I turned around, and there in front of the judges were Audrey, Max Sherman, and Emma, draped in giant robes. Audrey wore the spinner costume—the one we'd started making for Sierra. Emma, carrying a measuring stick, had my part—the Fate who determines how long people's lives will be. And Max wore Audrey's wig from two Halloweens ago, when she was Rapunzel. He was the wrinkly old Fate with scissors, who determines when people will die.

I grabbed Sierra's arm to steady myself.

Audrey hadn't gotten her way for once, so she'd stolen our costume idea—*Sierra's*, really—and twisted it around into exactly what she wanted.

"I can't believe she did that! Can you believe she did that?" I said.

Sierra shrugged, her shoulders pressing up into the bottom of her flower headpiece.

"Sit down!" somebody called to us. "We can't see."

So Sierra and I plopped down right where we were, in the middle of a bunch of sixth graders. And that's where we were still sitting when the eighth graders finished parading through and the judges stood up to announce the results.

Ms. Meadows stood up first and named the *Alice in Wonderland* crew the "Best Group Costume" winners. The sixth-grade girls jumped up and down, squealing, and then ran up to help themselves to prize candy. They're only a year younger than us, but they looked like little kids up there, bouncing around and hugging. I focused all my attention on the slightly crooked bottom of my Crayola sign to block out the memory of Audrey and me last year, leading the rest of our friends up to claim M&M's and Starbursts for our group costume prize.

Then Mr. Warren awarded the iPhone kid the prize for "Most Original Costume," and it was Mr. Ellis's turn. Ms. Meadows and Mr. Warren had used a microphone to talk loudly enough for everybody to hear them, but Mr. Ellis just projected.

"First of all, I want to thank the members of Worship and Ministry. They're working on some terrific initiatives to help us embrace simplicity, and the first step is today's Simplicity Prize, for a costume that's homemade instead of purchased. Worship and Ministry group, please stand so we can recognize you."

I stood and pulled Sierra up with me. Then she yanked me back down, but not before Jake caught my eye and gave me a giant grin.

"This is a tough decision," Mr. Ellis went on, "but since I'm a history teacher, you won't be surprised to know that I have a soft spot for Greek mythology."

Oh, no. No, no, no, please no.

"So the inaugural Simplicity Prize goes to Audrey Lee, Emma Walker, and the very lovely Max Sherman, a.k.a. the three Fates!"

Everybody clapped and hollered as Audrey, Emma, and Max went up to claim their prize—Mariah's homemade brownies. The three of them twirled and curtsied and held the brownies up in the air like trophies. I rubbed the soft fabric of Ryan's old shirt between my thumb and index finger, the way he must have done a million times when the shirt still fit him, even though what I wanted to do was to bang my fists against the gym floor. It was just so unfair.

Why is everything so unfair?

I yanked off my construction-paper crayon hat, but Sierra reached over to take it from me before I could crumple it up.

She took my hand and squeezed. I squeezed back, hard.

After the assembly—after the dance elective kids performed the "Thriller" dance and Mr. Ellis's advisory won the toilet-paper mummy-wrapping contest—I marched over to Audrey.

"Maybe it's better to let it go?" Sierra said as she followed me.

But there was no way I was just letting Audrey get away with what she'd done.

Audrey was standing with Max, who was eating his Simplicity Prize brownie and holding either Audrey's or Emma's.

He shifted both brownies to one hand and reached out to touch the top of Sierra's headpiece.

"What kind of flower are you? A daisy?" he asked.

Sierra ducked away, and I rolled my eyes. "Daisies have white petals, Max," I said. *And Sierra obviously doesn't want you flirting with her*, I wanted to add.

"Easy there, Loco," he said. That's what he started calling me last spring, Loco, as if he's calling me "crazy," since my first name sort of starts with a "Lo" sound, depending on how you say it, and my last name starts with the letters *Co*, even though that's not how the *o* sounds in Collins. And almost everyone who's from Philly says *Lauren* with a "La" sound, too.

"Um, the Gerber ones can be yellow, I think," Sierra said.

"But she's a sunflower," I told Max. Then I turned to Audrey. "And *you're* wearing Sierra's costume! The Fates were her idea!"

Audrey pretended to examine her robe and the string dangling from her hands. "I don't see her name on it anywhere. And I had to make most of it *by myself* after you two just left!"

"Only because you picked a fight with us!"

"Ladies, ladies," Max said, stepping in between us with his mouth full of brownie.

I leaned around him so I could look Audrey right in the eye. Aunt Jill was so right about her: always, always needing to get her way. "When we wouldn't give you every little thing you wanted, you stole our idea and found other people you could boss around."

"Hey!" Max protested.

I wasn't finished yet, though. "You don't deserve the Simplicity Prize, and you don't deserve me and Sierra."

Audrey gasped, and Max snapped his fingers and said, "Oh, no, she didn't!" in a high-pitched girly voice.

I took off out the gym door, with Sierra trailing behind me. I was right, and Audrey was wrong—I *knew* it. But somehow I felt worse after telling her so, not better.

Trick-or-treating is legendary in Mt. Airy, where we live. You have to walk down a bunch of blocks from our house to get to the really busy part, but Audrey and I have always gone, every year.

I'd told Sierra all about Mt. Airy Halloween—how many people are out, how much candy you can get—but after what happened at the assembly, I wasn't in the mood to go. And Sierra said she'd stay home with me.

"What would cheer you up?" she asked as we ate Chinese takeout in the kitchen.

We'd already ordered exactly what I wanted for dinner, and Mom had gone overboard at CVS, so we had a pretty unlimited supply of Halloween candy to dig into, but none of that was making me feel any better. I wasn't sure what would.

If Ryan were here, he would know. Ryan doesn't always understand other people's emotions, but somehow he's the best at figuring out how to fix things when you're sad. He sometimes needs Mom to tell him when I'm upset, but then he'll announce, "I'm going to cheer you up," and he really will.

The best was in fifth grade when I'd worked so hard practicing because I wanted this solo in our chorus concert. After I found out I didn't get it, Ryan let me pick the toppings on the pizza Mom ordered that night *and* choose the two best pieces.

Then he found the song on YouTube, listened to it until he learned it, and then played it by ear on our piano in the living room while I sang. He called Mom and Dad down to hear, and he told them, "Please listen to Lauren singing her song. You should applaud when it's over, but for Lauren's singing, not for how I play it on the piano." He even had Dad record it, so I could listen again anytime I felt sad.

"You're smiling," Sierra told me now. "That's a good sign, right?"

I felt sort of bad for Sierra, stuck inside on Halloween trying to make me feel better. So I said, "I'm good, yeah. And we can trick-or-treat together next year, I promise."

But she looked down at her Target brand sneakers and blinked too many times, and I realized: Sierra might not live here anymore next Halloween. She might be back with her parents, or whichever of them she used to live with. She probably *hoped* she'd be back with her parents, even though if I were choosing parents, I might pick Anne and Carl, with their old car and their hippie clothes and their easy smiles. Anne and Carl wouldn't have sent Ryan to boarding school. They lost their own daughter, back before I was born, so they always appreciate everybody else's kids. And they don't care about MacBook Airs and designer jeans and iPhones. I'm not sure they have a single TV in their whole house. They know what's important.

The idea of losing Sierra before next Halloween made my throat tighten up the way it does when I have a stomach bug and am about to throw up, and Dad had the living room TV blaring so loudly, it made my brain throb. I grabbed a bunch of Halloween candy and stood up.

"Let's go down to the basement."

It's my favorite part of our house these days because it reminds me of Ryan. Especially the calming corner Jenna helped us set up, with the old living room furniture and Ry's fish tank and lamps that aren't too bright.

"Whoa," Sierra said when she saw the fish tank.

It's pretty big—fifty-five gallons, instead of the five-gallon one he has at school—and it looks extra nice right now because Mom and Dad hired someone to clean it while Ryan's away, and the guy was just here. So the glass was clear, and the plants were bright green and stripped of the mossy algae that sometimes grows on them.

"It's my brother's," I told her. "He researches the different kinds of fish that can live together, and he sets up the plants and rocks so they can all have their own little places to hide if they need to be by themselves. He loves it."

Sierra took a seat on the couch that faces the tank. "They're pretty," she said. "I like the red and blue ones."

"Cardinal tetras, they're called," I told her.

"It's relaxing, isn't it? Watching them?"

I sat down next to her. "Yeah. It calms Ryan, watching them float around. And the sound of the water does too, I think."

It sort of calms me, too, lately. Except looking at the fish tank also reminds me that it's been a little while since I got a video message from Ry. He sent one more after I filmed the fish the other week, but it was a video of him petting one of the horses and brushing its long brown mane, and he was smiling and he sounded pretty happy and everything . . . but I can't imagine he really was. I was in those horse stables over Family Weekend, and I know how gross they smelled. And he hasn't responded to my last message, when I showed him my Halloween costume and played him part of the song we're singing in music class.

I guess I should have specifically told him to send me another one back, because he might not realize I'm expecting him to. But I never had to say that when I was at camp. He did it on his own because he wanted to.

Mom keeps saying it's different now that *he's* the one away, but I still don't know.

Sierra and I tore into fun-size Twix bars, Snickers, and Milky Ways, leaving the wrappers in a pile on the floor.

"What are those two doing?" she asked, pointing at the two big angelfish, who kept swimming right at each other and then darting away.

"They hate each other," I said. "They're both males. There used to be a female one, and they used to fight over her." Then I laughed. "I told Ry I thought maybe they could put aside their differences and be friends after she died, and he was like, 'I need you to stop anthropomorphizing my fish, please, Lauren.'"

That was after he'd been working with Jenna for a while. She was helping him figure out how to speak up and say what he needed before he got really overwhelmed. It's still really hard for him to do it—Jenna said it's a process to develop that skill—but that time, he did. Mom was there, and she was so busy praising Ryan for asking for what he wanted that I don't think she even heard me ask what the word meant.

"Anthropo-what?" Sierra asked.

"Right?" I said. "It means treating them like they're human when they're not—I had to look it up."

"Ryan sounds smart," Sierra said.

"He's super-smart," I told her. "He loves science and history, and he's so amazing at music that he can hear a song and then play it on the piano without reading music."

Sierra crinkled a Twix wrapper between her fingers. "That's really cool. Maybe I'll get to meet him someday."

"When he comes home at Christmas," I said. Almost two whole months away.

"Yeah," Sierra said. "Christmas."

She flinched as those two male angelfish swam right at each other again, and I realized—that might be awful for her, the idea of being here for Christmas instead of wherever she usually is.

So I handed her the last Snickers and changed the subject. "What did you dress up as for Halloween last year?"

She wasn't wearing the flower headpiece anymore, but she still had on my green jeans, rolled up a little so they wouldn't be too long, and her green T-shirt. They were close to the same color but not quite. I wondered how many spots away from each other those two greens would be if they were in Audrey's giant box of markers, still organized by shade because she hasn't used them enough to mix them up.

"I didn't dress up last year," Sierra said.

But there was something about the way her eyes darted around that made me wonder if she was telling the truth. I followed her eyes to the right of the couch, then the left, and caught a glimpse of something shiny on the ground, just peeking out from behind the leg of the end table.

I walked over, leaned down, and picked up Mom's ring: swirly strands of silver coiled into a thick band, with a big honey-colored stone rimmed with gold. She always wears her wedding rings on her left hand, but she used to wear this one on her right sometimes. Audrey's mom has a bracelet that looks like it: coiled silver rimmed with gold, and two stones in the center. And Mom went all shrill and gushy when Dad gave her the ring for her birthday once. That means it's expensive. But she hasn't worn it for ages. She must have lost it a long time ago. She's probably stopped looking for it by now.

I thought of Audrey's cuff bracelet stashed at the bottom of the blue plastic bin on the other side of the room with the three hundred dollars from the jeans and the jersey, just waiting to be delivered to Jenna.

Sierra hugged her knees to her chest and leaned into the arm of the sofa.

She has to know the unfairness of everything as well as I do—better, even. It was her idea that Audrey stole, and I saw the way she froze when we first walked into Audrey's house and again when she saw our big TV in the living room, and our dining room with Mom's crystal candlesticks sparkling. And even though she won't talk much about her parents or where she used to live, I looked up Uncle Al's Bar & Grill from that shirt she wears, so I know what town she's from. "An impoverished area" is how Mom would describe it.

I took a deep breath. "There's something I want to show you."

I dug Audrey's bracelet out of the old puzzle bin, because it doesn't matter anymore that she used to be nice to Ryan and come up with the most fun plans for the two of us. I held the bracelet up next to Mom's ring, and they both glistened under the soft light from Ryan's lamps.

"This is gonna sound weird at first, but I have this plan."

And I told her. About what everything has been like since Mom and Dad sent Ryan away, and all the stuff they've been buying, and what Jenna had said, about people who couldn't afford enough OT sessions. And the jeans and the jersey, and how Mom and Audrey didn't need this jewelry—they didn't even care that it was gone.

"I could use some help, if you're interested," I told Sierra, because I thought it might make her feel better, doing *something* even if it wouldn't fix *everything*. "You could just help with looking out for more stuff people don't need that I can sell. And getting to the post office to mail stuff if my parents start getting suspicious."

Sierra didn't say anything for a long time. I'm an expert in the meaning of all of Audrey's expressions, but I couldn't read the look on Sierra's face.

"It just isn't right," I said. "That some people have so much and others have so little. This is . . . it's one way I can start to make things fair."

Sierra sat up a little straighter and nodded. "Yeah. I'll help you."

And even though Audrey was probably out trick-or-treating with Emma and Max Sherman, and even though Ryan was gone, I grinned and reached my hand out for Sierra to shake.

"Partners in . . ." *Crime* wasn't quite right, though. *Mischief*? Not exactly. But then I got it. "Partners in justice."

"Partners in justice," she said back.

SIERRA

Mixed Up

I come home from Lauren's
wishing I could have one of her TVs
and forget
all of what she just told me.

I'm the only one who knows her secret.

It means she really trusts me.
More than anyone right now, maybe.

Which makes us almost more like family than friends.

I lie on my bed,
look into my kaleidoscope.
A science teacher told me once
there are three mirrors in a kaleidoscope.
It's not just the colors that matter, it's the mirrors, he said.

Now I wonder
if colors are what guide your day, maybe
the mirrors are like the people who matter.
Mom, Lauren,
reflecting your mood, back to you.

If Lauren's happy about this plan,
then I should be, too.

Structure

Mr. Ellis says
he needs to see me about my report.
Says it is very good
that I make strong inferences.
Not sure what that means.
He says he can tell I'm a deep thinker.
This I get.
I nod.
But he asks if I ever learned how to structure
an essay.
I think back—
so many school days Mom dropped me
    at the mall, the movies, so she could drink
    or other days she said she was sick,
    I had to skip school
    to take care of her.
  All I see is her,
    glassy eyes, tipsy smile,
when he asks me about the structure of an essay.
I shake my head, he says we will work on it.
"And one more thing," he says.
My heart skipping beats.
Scared suddenly—
he knows about my family,
he's going to ask me about her.
I sigh, relieved, when all he says is
next time,
make sure my essay's typed.

Before Blue

Lauren walks me home.
       I can feel her mood is up,
           so mine follows it,
           like an escaped balloon.
Asks if I can sleep over on Saturday,
wonder if she will let me watch one of her TVs.
Most Saturday nights at Mom's, I would watch
marathons of whatever was on,
eat leftover Chinese,
frozen pizza.
Sometimes Cassidy would join me.
Tell Lauren I can't wait. Wave.
Almost ask her to take me with her.
When I'm with Lauren   I forget sometimes
       to miss Mom,
       to feel annoyed with Anne,
       confused by Carl.
Inside, I pet Seeger, try
to go straight to my room
but Carl stops me.
Home from an early shift.

He sits me down, says
Mr. Ellis called, that I need to start
working on the computer at home.
He says it like he should've thought of that already,
says before they've mostly fostered younger kids.

Looking past him,
I wonder for a minute
all the colors my room's been

before blue.

A Space for Me

Carl shows me the office.
It's a wonder they can find anything in there.
    Papers everywhere,
    old art projects,
    dust.
He moves things around.
    Makes a space for me.
        He calls it my "workstation."
        Like he's hired me, like he's proud.
I tell him thanks.
Because even though it smells kind of moldy,
and it is full of plants and boxes,
the computer itself is silver and shiny,
and when I power it on,
for a minute
I can't help but feel
greener, luckier.

Like Mom would smile,
if she was looking on.

Her Face

With the computer, I log on to Mom's Facebook.
So I can see her.
     The selfies with new hairdos,
     her and me before the movies,
     her with our old kitten Cameron.
     Her and Lena on their trip to Atlantic City.
     One of our plastic Christmas trees.

I touch my finger to each picture,
like maybe she can feel me close.

Museums

On the bus the next day I tell Lauren
about the office and
then ask her about the secret room.
She says Anne and Carl's daughter died
before we were even born.

They've kept that room like that so long?

Like how Mr. Ellis says a culture hangs on to its history
by building museums.
Building museums is a part of human nature.

If one of my parents was gone forever,
        I wonder
if I would try to make a space
        that was just theirs
or if I would just keep a room for each of them
        in my mind.

The Spirit of the Day

Lauren and I head to our Worship & Ministry meeting,
work on how to get kids excited about the Simplicity-a-Thon.

Two fifth-grade girls have joined now,
because they liked one of Lauren's posters
and the simplicity costume prize.
> They both have braces
> and matching silver glitter temporary tattoos on
> > their hands,
> > > something Mom and I once did at the mall.

Lauren, next to me
but she's also next to Jake,
who keeps scribbling on her paper
and stealing her fries.
I wonder if she notices
how his dark eyes
watch her even when she's quiet
how he makes a point to let his hand linger by her side?

> If Nan were here, she'd tell Lauren
> not to mess with *a boy like that.*
> She wouldn't have said exactly what she meant,
> like when I was friends with Alex from the third
> > apartment complex
> and she told me *not to go over to a place like that.*

Mom would always tell me not to listen to Nan,
she would always let me go over there.
If she were here, she'd tell
Lauren now:
Pay attention, girl, he likes you.

The group votes to do the Simplicity-a-Thon
the Tuesday before Thanksgiving
"in the spirit of the day."

      Last Thanksgiving,
      Mom let me visit Dad
      for ten minutes
      before going to her new boyfriend's.
      Dad looked pale, greasy.
      He had drawn a picture for me.
      A cartoon of us walking our old mutt Mr. Little.

Now Lauren seems mad at something.
I can tell from her face
and the way my stomach flips.
On the way out, I ask her what's wrong.
My voice shakes a bit,
worried I did something.

She says Thanksgiving is actually a lie.
That the Indians were slaughtered by Europeans.
And we celebrate like everything's all about turkey and gravy.
She says she's mad that that even happened at all.

I take her hand again and say
we're going to do something good that week.
The Simplicity-a-Thon,
something she made up all her own.

I tell her she should be
proud
not
sad.

But maybe there's something else wrong.
Maybe like Nan, it's what
she *isn't* saying
that really matters.

Island

The next day,
      in the cafeteria line,
Audrey pokes me with her tray.
      Says it isn't on purpose.
But I know better.
      I want to tell her
I know what it is like to lose people.

That I know Lauren might still be hers
      if I wasn't here.

But no one says stuff like that aloud.
And she did make things worse.
Tempting the Fates.
Instead I join Lauren,
               just the two of us,
               our own island
               her old friends
a   churning
sea   away.

The Questions Underneath

At the sleepover, I flip on the TV.
Lauren goes to get us some sodas.
When she comes back,
asks what I'm doing.
My stomach flips.
                I turn it off.

Lauren's smile grows as she tells me
about the jewelry.
Someone's bought the bracelet
but not the ring—
                not yet.

Later, underneath a crystal chandelier,
we eat take-out Thai food.
Her parents
are nice to me during dinner,
but I think they're being polite,
wondering probably about Audrey.

That night,
Lauren and I stay up late,
laughing, playing with her Magic 8 Ball.
Asking it questions no one
could ever predict.

Will one of us get sick the Tuesday after next?
Will Max take Emma to prom when we are seniors?

We giggle into the night.

As we fall asleep,
I think how in some ways being with Lauren
feels like being with Cassidy,
like we are inventing our own world.

But Cassidy always
joked us out of our problems.

Lauren is the opposite,
she names a problem, then

tries to solve it.

Watch Her Watch

In the morning,
Lauren says we're going to take a walk.
I ask can we go to CVS.
She shrugs but doesn't say no.
We walk the aisles.
>   I smell Mom's old Suave shampoo.
>   Trace my finger on the edge of a tissue box.
>   Scan the candy, in the order I've memorized.
All CVSs the same.
>   Sober Mom would get her nicotine gum,
>   her energy shots,
>   I would finger magazines,
>   palm the holiday decorations.
In the aisle now, Halloween on sale, Christmas already
    begun,
Lauren holds a snow globe.
>   Watch her watch the spinning snow.
We scan the makeup.
Lauren says she and Audrey used to practice with it
>   but she's given it up.
She's not going to
"succumb to corporate greed telling us what's beautiful."
Says isn't it ridiculous
how some of this makeup costs so much?
Just this drugstore makeup?

I wonder
　　　as she stands there so long
　　　hovering over eye shadows, cover-up, lipstick,
　　　if she's actually going to maybe take it,
　　　not pay for it.
Does she think CVS is doing something wrong, too?
I look at the security cameras, the doors.
Wonder then—
like I still have that 8 Ball in my hand—

If she took it, would I turn her in?

Innocent

But
she
doesn't
take
a
thing.

The
security
mirror
watches
us
go.

Pockets

On our way home,
Lauren points, says that's Emma's house.
There's a yard sale outside
old Barbies,
Pokémon cards,
jewelry,
scarves.
She makes chitchat
with Emma's mother,
but when Emma's mother turns,
she swipes some cuff links.
I poke her when Emma's mom
turns back around. On the way home
she says that Emma's family's so wealthy,
  they shouldn't have yard sales,
  they should just donate.

I feel the cuff links
heavy now in my own pocket
as if I was the one who stole them.

Shut Out

When I get home from the sleepover,
I feel tired.
Realize it's Sunday again.
Mom better call.
Anne says she heard from the social worker.
Mom's still in jail
but not for much longer.
Her evaluation period's almost over.
Then Anne says she won't let me
stay up late again, waiting.
"It is not going to happen."
I ask her why not.

She says I can't wait around for someone
who might not show up.
That it isn't fair to me.
Who is she to say anything about my mom?
What does she know?

I say:
"You're the one who keeps a room for someone who's never
      showing up again."

As soon as I say it, I can't believe I have.
Carl looks sideways at Anne, whose tears are already coming.
He says I need to go to my room, no dinner,
that if my mom calls, he will come get me.

Asks don't I know the word *respect*?

As I climb the stairs,
Seeger follows.
But I tell him to scram.
He cries as I

shut him
out.

Switch Places

I text Cassidy then
       tell her let's
       meet up soon.
Tell her I hate it here
       I just want to be back home.
She says: She wishes
       she could switch places with me
       like *Freaky Friday*,
       her sisters are snoring,
       there wasn't enough pizza at dinner,
       and my new school sounds kind of awesome.

As usual, no matter how bad things are,
            she makes me laugh.
But underneath I squish down another feeling.
One that wants to yell at her:
       I'm not lucky!
         Neither of my parents can take care of me.
Before I can get angrier, she distracts me again.
Asks if there are any cute boys at Quaker schools.
Max's teasing smile flashes at me.
Is that how he acts with everyone?
Hard to imagine a boy actually liking me.
And who cares, I am just here temporarily.

So, I just tell her no,
not a chance,
no way.

LAUREN

Consequences

Ever since the weekend, Sierra's had dark circles under her eyes. She says everything's fine, but she's been staring off into space a lot or doodling with her head hunched over her notebook. And at the end of the day today, she was standing by herself outside Ms. Meadows's classroom when I went to get my stuff, and I had to say her name twice before she saw me.

"I was waiting for you," she said. "I can't come to your field hockey game. I'm so sorry."

The hallway was full of end-of-the-day chaos—kids laughing and shouting and shoving one another—but all that faded into background static. "What is it? What happened?"

I was afraid it was something with her parents—like something bad had happened, or it was already time for her to leave Anne and Carl's and go back to them.

Mom talked to me the other day, after Sierra slept over. She said how nice Sierra is, how happy she is that Sierra and I are friends. She said she knows three can be a hard number and sometimes friends like Audrey and me need some time apart, and that's okay. But then, right when I thought the conversation was over, she added, "You know what it means that

Sierra's in foster care, right? You remember how those little boys stayed with Anne and Carl for a while but then they left?"

And I said of course I know and told her I had to finish homework because I didn't want to think about Sierra leaving, but I kept thinking about it anyway. So now I was worried she was going to go back to her home from before and worried that it made me a bad friend that I didn't want her to.

Sierra looked down at her sneakers. "Mr. Ellis says I have to stay and work with him on essay structure."

I almost laughed, I was so relieved.

"I know it's your last game of the season, and I promised . . ." she started.

I'd told her how I was sort of missing Ryan's good-luck notes and how Mom was babysitting my cousin Melody, so she couldn't come.

"It's fine, Sierra! Don't worry! It's just field hockey. It doesn't matter, OK?"

She gave me a shaky nod, and I walked her to Mr. Ellis's room before I went to the locker room to change.

As I lined up at left wing for the beginning of the game, I tried to remember what I'd told her: *It's just field hockey. It doesn't matter.*

So no one was there to watch me. And so Audrey and Emma were huddled together at the end of the bench whispering. What difference did that make, in the grand scheme of things?

Our team had the ball to start, so as soon as the eighth grader playing center forward tapped it to the right wing, I sprinted up the field to get open. Pretty soon, the ball came my way, and I ran toward it, reaching out my stick to tap it away from my defender. I dribbled a few steps and smacked a flat pass to the center forward, and someone on the sideline yelled, "Go, Lauren!"

"Atta girl, Laur!" somebody else shouted. Dad?

Once the ball went out of bounds, I glanced over at the bleachers. Jake was in the front row with a bunch of eighth-grade boys, wearing a green fleece and giving me a thumbs-up. And two rows behind him was Dad, still in his navy work suit and long coat. Dad saw me looking and waved.

I took off back down the field to help on defense, feeling an extra charge in my legs.

And the thing is, I know it doesn't *really* matter that I scored a goal and we won the game 2–1—not the way it matters that some of Jenna's clients can't afford their sessions, or that Sierra can't live with her parents, or that Ryan doesn't live with us. But it still felt pretty excellent to hear people cheer for me when I launched the ball into the back of the net and to high-five all my teammates when the ref blew the final whistle. Except for Audrey, who only got into the game for five minutes and stood off to the side by herself.

And then after the game, when I sat down in the front seat of Dad's car, things felt more right than they had in a while. Just the two of us, talking sports like we used to, except he had more to say about my field hockey shot than how the Eagles' season was going. We hadn't had any Dad-and-Lauren time at all since Ryan left. Mom and I eat dinner, just the two of us, whenever Dad works late. But it's never just Dad and me anymore. Mom comes along for everything.

And, yeah, Dad chose box seats over upper level at the

Eagles' game. He cares about things that aren't important, and he never really talks to me about Ryan, so all of that's completely messed up. But he was acting like he still cared about *me* in the car after the game. If he was ever going to listen, maybe now was the time.

So when we stopped at a red light, I said, "Dad? I really miss Ry."

I thought of what Mom had said the other day, about three being a hard number—how I knew she was talking about me and Audrey and Sierra, but it's true for her and Dad and me, too.

"Oh, Lauren," he said. "I know. I miss him so much, too."

And his voice was gentle, and his eyes were sad, so I went for it.

"I've been thinking . . . maybe we could all go to North Carolina for Thanksgiving? I have three days off school, and it just wouldn't be right, you know? To have Thanksgiving without Ryan?"

I'd even looked up restaurants near the Piedmont school, and there's one that's supposed to be calm and cozy according to the reviews, and they have home-style mashed potatoes on the menu—Ry's favorite. I thought maybe we could have Thanksgiving there, just the four of us, or else we could pick up food from there and eat it in our hotel room. And if it was just the four of us, away from the school for a little bit, maybe Ry would admit that he wants to come home.

The light changed to green, and Dad started to drive. He drove around a bend and leaned over to look behind my seat so he could change lanes. Then, finally, he took in a big breath.

"Sweetheart, that's a nice idea. It really is. But Christmas is coming up so soon, and flights are so expensive over Thanksgiving weekend."

My adrenaline spiked, the same way it had when I yelled at Audrey on Halloween. "So?"

He can shell out money for meaningless electronics, but it isn't a priority to pay for flights to spend a holiday with his *son*? Yeah, Thanksgiving's a lie, and I don't have any desire to celebrate the Pilgrims slaughtering the Indians, but when everybody else has a giant meal with family, I don't want Ryan in North Carolina by himself, and I don't want the three of us at home acting like he doesn't exist.

Dad smoothed a hand over his hair, which is thinning a little on top, and switched back into the left lane. "Mom and I were planning to talk to you about this soon, but Mom's going down to North Carolina for a few days, to have Thanksgiving dinner at the school and see some of Ryan's classes."

"Just Mom's going?"

Dad had to stop at another red light, but he refused to look at me. He spun his gold wedding ring around on his finger and then rubbed his left temple, as if I was giving him a headache.

"We've thought about it and talked to Ryan's OT at school," he said, finally, when the light turned green and he started to drive.

Ugh. Smug Scott. "You didn't talk to *me*!" I said. "You never talk to me at all!"

"We're trying our hardest here, Lauren!" Dad snapped. Then he took another deep breath as he made a left turn, and his voice was softer when he spoke again. "I'm sorry, sweetheart. It's just that it'll be a calmer holiday for Ry if he only has one visitor. And then maybe we can all go back down in the spring, once . . . well, once things are more settled."

"And once the flights aren't so expensive, since you're suddenly so worried about money?" I spat out.

He sighed. "It's not really the money, Laur. I know it was tough on you, too, going down for Family Weekend."

I pinched the scratchy fabric of my field hockey skirt and thought how much Ryan would hate the way it feels. "You think it's less tough on me to keep me away from Ryan?"

Dad didn't answer. "We'll bring Ryan home for his whole two-week winter break before you know it," he said instead. "You and I get to go to Aunt Jill and Aunt Becky's, like always. I bet you can convince them to make a cherry pie if you ask nicely."

He smiled at me as we pulled onto our street. As if the promise of cherry pie was going to fix everything. As if going to Aunt Jill and Aunt Becky's will somehow be the same as always when Ryan and Mom won't be there.

"It's easier for Ryan this way, Laur, to have a holiday that's a little more low-key," he added when I didn't fall all over myself in delight. "And it'll be easier for you if we visit him in the spring instead, when he's even more settled. I promise."

He said "easier for Ryan" and "easier for me." But he obviously meant easier for him and Mom.

When we pulled up in front of our house, I got out before Dad even turned off the car, and I slammed the door behind me.

And later, before I went to bed, I swiped Dad's Fitbit from his study. He bought it at least a month ago, when he decided he wanted to get in better shape, but he hasn't even taken it out of the box. I stuffed it inside the old puzzle bin, lowered the price on Mom's swirly ring online, and listed the Fitbit for sale, too.

I was too amped up to focus on my homework until it was late, which meant I fell asleep in the middle of my history reading and had to scramble to finish in the morning. Mr. Ellis gives us pop quizzes sometimes, and I didn't want to fail.

Anyway, it's not like Mom does much of anything during the day lately, so I figured it'd be no problem to ask her for a ride if I missed the bus. But when I was ready to go, I couldn't find her.

I checked everywhere I could think of: her and Dad's room, Dad's study, even outside. And then I heard something thud down in the basement.

I tore down the stairs, and there she was, crouched down to pick up a plastic storage bin filled with a bunch of my old dolls. She moved it to the middle of the room, where most of the bins were already sitting. She'd already moved the blue one with the puzzles.

I told my voice it had to sound normal. "What are you doing, Mom?"

She raised her eyebrows. "What are *you* doing? Shouldn't you be at the bus stop?"

"I had to finish some homework. I was hoping maybe you could drive me?"

She looked down at her dusty hands and wiped them on her jeans. "This isn't the best morning, hon. I have painters coming at nine. That's why I have to move everything away from the walls. We're finally freshening up the paint down here—it's been ages."

I looked around, at Ryan's calming corner and the familiar old furniture. "But I love this room."

She bent back down to straighten the top of the doll bin, which had come off when she moved the box. "I bet you'll love it even more once it's gotten a fresh coat of paint!"

"What about Ryan's corner?" I squeaked. "What about the fish?"

"We'll keep all that just like it is," she said. "The painters said they can reach the wall behind the tank with their special rollers without disrupting anything. I'll just get rid of some of this clutter, and Dad thinks we should put a pool table on this side where all the storage was. That'd be fun, right?"

But I didn't have room in my brain to think about a pool table because I was stuck on the word *clutter* and the idea of the top of the doll bin coming off. Other bins could come open, too, or she could start sorting the stuff in them. "Wha . . . what are you getting rid of?"

"I have no idea yet, babe. I don't even know what's in most of these bins. But I won't give anything away without checking with you, OK?"

As if *that's* what I was worried about.

Mom checked her watch. "If we leave right now, I can take you. I'll just grab my purse."

I followed her up the basement stairs, but when she veered off to get her purse, I tiptoed back down to rescue the ring and Fitbit and cuff links and money—$340 now that I'd sold Audrey's bracelet, too—in case she started decluttering today. I sprinted up to my room with them.

"Lauren! We need to go now!" Mom yelled up to me.

So I shoved the stuff into my pajama drawer and then ran back down the stairs and out the door, which Mom was already holding open.

At the end of the day, Sierra and I took the bus home together. We can both take the early bus now that field hockey is over. She was listening to her headphones when I got on, and she took them out once I sat down next to her, but then she didn't say anything.

"Is everything OK?" I asked her again once we got off at our stop.

She nodded, like she had every other time I'd asked.

"You know you can talk to me if something's up, right?" I said. "Or I can look at your history essay for you, if you're stressed about it."

She nodded and said, "Thanks." And I hope that's really all that's bothering her—Mr. Ellis's essay assignment. And that she really will talk to me if it's something more, so I can listen and try to help.

"Well, text me if you want company walking Seeger later, OK?"

She said sure and smiled, but it was the fake kind. I was trying to think of something to say to make her smile for real, but before I could come up with anything, she gave me a little wave and headed up the path to her house.

So I went inside my house, too, and I was walking toward the kitchen to get a snack, but Dad's voice stopped me.

"Lauren. Come in here, please."

It was way too early for him to be home from work, but there he was in the living room—he and Mom both, right next to each other on the smaller sofa. They never sit on that one, since the bigger one faces the TV.

"Sit down, Lauren," Mom said.

And the worst part is, what popped into my mind was: *They changed their minds about Thanksgiving. They want to apologize about their ridiculous plan and tell me of course all three of us are going to North Carolina so we can be together as a family.*

But then, as I sat on the edge of the long couch, which could have fit six of me side by side by side, I looked over at them. And the expressions on their faces—they were worse than the disappointed frowns I used to dread. Sad and stern and . . . worried. They'd never looked worried about me before. I wasn't the one they worried about.

Before they said anything, Dad glanced down toward the coffee table, and when I followed his gaze there, my mouth went dry.

The Fitbit, still in its box. Mom's ring, with the honey-colored stone shining. The cuff links from Emma's family's yard sale. A stack of money.

The first thing I thought was how small the stack of bills looked. How much less than $340 I would have guessed there was, if I hadn't already known.

"Do you want to explain why I found all that in your pajama drawer?" Mom said.

It was hard to swallow with my mouth so dry, but I managed. "Do *you* want to explain why you were going through my stuff?"

I knew it was the wrong thing to say even as I said it. Now I couldn't backtrack and pretend I had no idea where any of it had come from. But it still gave me an adrenaline jolt, watching Mom's mouth open into an O.

"I thought I'd put your laundry away for you, since I had time, and I—"

Dad put a hand on Mom's knee to stop her from saying anything more.

"Your mother is not the one on trial here, Lauren Elizabeth."

I was, in other words.

"You've *stolen* from your mother and me and someone else, too, by the look of things. What else did you take, Lauren? Where did all this money come from, and what could you possibly need it for?"

"Are you in some kind of trouble?" Mom added. "Are you buying . . . something you couldn't ask us to pay for?"

"No!" I shouted.

What did they think, that I was on *drugs* or something? Mom looked panicked, but Dad's eyes had turned hard and disapproving. He was looking at me the way he probably looks at the corrupt jerks he prosecutes in the courtroom in his white-collar-crime cases.

But how is that fair, to look at me like I'm some kind of criminal when I'm trying to do something *good*?

"The money is for *charity*!" There was no way they'd understand if I told them the truth, but another explanation came to me. "It's for the Simplicity-a-Thon, at school. I told you about it already. That's money I've gotten from sponsors."

Mom exhaled as she sank back into her seat.

Dad nodded slowly, but I couldn't tell if he believed me or not. "And the other things?"

"The cuff links are Sierra's," I said. "She . . . we bought them at a yard sale last weekend. They're for her dad. For when she gets to see him again. She didn't want to bring them to Anne and Carl's because she doesn't want to hurt their feelings. And the stuff that's yours . . ."

I looked up at the giant TV hanging on the wall in front of me. Dad bought it over Memorial Day weekend last spring, claiming there was such a huge sale, it would have been silly *not* to, even though there was nothing wrong with our old TV at all.

I thought back to the time Audrey's parents had caught us charging neighbor kids five bucks each to enter our Hamster and Guinea Pig Obstacle Course Race. Audrey had gotten them down from super-mad to medium mad by telling them we were trying to earn money so I could buy Ryan a new fish for his birthday. That was part of the truth, but the rest of it was that we also wanted the purple flower-patterned sunglasses her mom thought were tacky.

Maybe there was a way to tell Mom and Dad part of the truth now, too?

"I don't like the way you buy all this expensive stuff that doesn't matter. You send me to a school where we talk all about simplicity, but then it doesn't feel like we're living very simply at all."

"So you took things from us to teach us a lesson?" Dad asked.

"I don't know. I guess sort of. I found them and didn't even know if you would look for them. I wanted to see if you noticed they were gone."

Mom and Dad exchanged a long look, and Dad let out a loud sigh.

"That was way over the line, Lauren. Sneaky and completely inappropriate."

His voice wasn't as sharp as it had been a minute ago, though. He was softening.

"It's great that you take these Quaker values seriously, but you have to talk to us if something's bothering you," he added.

As if *that* had any chance at working.

They made me go upstairs while they decided on my consequences: no TV and no iPhone for the next two weeks.

I don't even care that much about the punishment, but I do care that somebody finally bought Mom's ring and I had to give back the money, since I don't have it anymore. I can't take a chance on taking any more stuff around the house or hiding anything here. But how much good can $340 do?

Back up in my room, I looked at that old photo of all four of us after my lower school graduation again, and then I paged through the notebook full of "Ryan Triggers" I'd started keeping because Jenna had taught us to log the causes of Ryan's meltdowns so we could figure out triggers he couldn't really explain.

Mom says she typed up all the triggers and shared them with the Piedmont school, but I bet Scott the Smug OT hasn't read them. I bet he doesn't have any idea that it upsets Ryan if you try to give his fish people names, like Archie the Angelfish and Nina the Neon Tetra. Or that Ryan hates it if you sit in the wrong seat at the kitchen table, or that socks grate against his ankles and heels if they lose their elastic and slide too far down.

And I bet he has no idea how Ryan loves to set up special hiding places for his shy fish, behind rocks and plants. Or how easily he can remember dates and facts about history, even if he just hears them once. Or how he really likes to play classical music on the piano, but he plays songs from Mom's favorite musicals and my favorite Disney movies, too, because he knows how happy it makes us to sing along.

I thought of Jenna, who understood all those things about Ryan. Who beamed at me when she told me what a helpful sister I am. Who keeps trying as hard as she can for all her clients even though it must make her furious how unfair it is, that she can't help people like Hailey as much as she wants to.

If Jenna can keep trying even though she has so many obstacles to deal with, I can, too, even though now it's going to be harder. I just need Sierra to help me figure out how.

SIERRA

Slide Closer

When I come into my room,
Anne is there.
She asks if I'm going to start to unpack.
Says living out of a suitcase
is harder
than it would be to use some drawers.
I don't tell her
that I had unpacked a bit
but then we fought
and I put most of it back in.
Now she sits on my bed.
　　　I slide closer to the window.
I don't know why she's talking to me,
　　　after I said such a mean thing to her.
Says she wants to explain.
Why she keeps her room—
　　　Amy's room—
set up.
Tell her I don't really care.
　　　Which isn't true, but

I want it to be.
Says it's because
  she wants to always remember her
    the way she was
      when she was happy.
I nod, watch Seeger in the yard
chasing his tail,
I'm not sure what to say.
I realize I don't even know
how Amy died.
Biting my tongue,
  I don't ask her what I want to know:
    When she says she was happy,
    does she mean Anne or Amy?

What Never Grew

Carl, happy that Anne & I spoke,
knocks on my door,
shows me his garden map.
      It is a grid on graph paper.
      Different symbols for different vegetables.
He says he won't ever plant tomatoes again
where he did last year,
too much "blossom end rot."
And he is going to have to do better with
"the whiteflies attacking the kale."
He's going to try using some "diluted Dr. Bronner's" to kill
    the pests.
I don't really understand anything he's saying
or why he's showing me the map.

He keeps explaining,
pointing out my window.
Showing me how each square on the map
represents a place in the actual garden.

Then, he coughs and says
he will learn from his mistakes
and start again in early spring.
He says he's been thinking of my question
about why he grows his own food,
why he works so hard.

He has a better answer:
        He likes to watch
        the cycle of life.
        To participate in it.

He says some of building relationships is about
        creation & destruction.

        And that understanding this,
        watching this cycle,
        helped him accept the loss of Amy.

        Is that why he's come up here? To tell me that?

I think of last spring,
how Mom promised to plant a garden.
As a favor to our landlady.
A way to help with one month's rent.

She tried turning the patch of grass
        into a garden by just
                pouring soil on top of it
        and then
                planting tomatoes, cucumbers, peppers.
I kept telling her
it might not work
she might need to water, read instructions.

Just like her plants
                    creating, destroying
            her promises
                    never took.
I look back at all of Carl's plans.
Down at his well-loved garden.

Imagine it in springtime.
Imagine it helping him.

But—

            not sure what that has to do with me,
            not sure whether I care   .
            about his garden

            growing.

Back to Himself

We go outside, Carl tells me it's time
I learned more about compost.

"What's your father like, Sierra?" Carl asks
        as he shows me how to put the dead leaves,
        over the just-dumped compost.

                        It was Mom
                        who turned Dad in.
                        She *ratted on him*
                        he said, Tammy said.
                        I said she did him a favor.
                            Maybe in prison
                he would be clean
                maybe in there
                he could get back
                to his drawings,
                his books, cooking,
                to himself.
                        Maybe jail has helped Mom, too?

"He's an artist," I tell Carl,
covering the yellowed apple cores,
leftover noodles,
coffee grounds,
with the brown, dry leaves.

Proof

The next day,
Mr. Ellis and I have another meeting after school
to talk about the structure of an essay.
He says:
You must have a thesis statement
then take examples from the text
and prove it.
You have to restate your introduction
in your conclusion.
I think of Lauren
     how sure she is
          of what she wants
               to say, do.
I go back and forth
between three statements
on the American Revolution.

Mr. Ellis says
what's important isn't in the choosing,
it's in the proving.

Charity

At Worship & Ministry,
they debate over where to send the money raised
from the Simplicity-a-Thon.
Jake says
       Habitat for Humanity,
Mariah says
       World Wildlife Fund.
Lauren
       turns to me
          and says,
             what about a place
                that gives
                   to foster kids?
My cheeks burn hot
like when Cassidy called my dad
a criminal in front of the teacher
last year.
       How could she do that?
       Bring all that attention to me?
I run out of the room,
past rows of L.L. Bean backpacks
a lost & found full of brand-new ski jackets.

I don't need her charity.

People Who Deserve It

Lauren chases after me
says she's so sorry,
didn't mean to embarrass me.
Just wanted to give money
        to people who really deserve it
        not to houses or the planet
        but right to people.
She tries to hug me.
I shrug her off.

Above us a display,
historical Quaker quotes.
One reads:
You Lift Me &
I'll Lift Thee &
We'll Ascend Together.
It makes me think how Lauren & I
have both cheered each other up
at different times.
        Mr. Ellis said proving matters more than choosing.
I realize
as I step back toward Lauren:
It isn't Lauren's choice to be my friend
that's the most surprising
but how far she's gone—
chasing after me, losing Audrey—

to prove it.

Just Because

I tell her   it's okay
I don't want her to be friends with me
      because
      she thinks
      I need help.
She tells me
that is not at all the reason.
Says, hey, let's do something fun this weekend.
Says her parents will drop us
at the movies by the mall.
If only she knew
how well I knew
that mall.
She might not want to take me there at all.

But I say yes,
thinking maybe
being with her there
might turn all that orange,
yellow.

Overfilled

I text Cassidy
to see if she could meet us there.
Imagine:
>Lauren laughing at Cassidy's jokes.
>Cassidy admiring Lauren's face and hair.
>Trying to up each other, dare for dare.

But she says she can't get a ride,
her mom had to take the twins to the Urgent Care.
Both up all night with coughs.

Lauren and I, in Aveda,
smelling shampoos,
>chamomile, rosemary & mint.
I always wondered how
people could pay that much money to wash their hair.
Think of Cassidy's coughing sisters.
How much it will cost Lena to take care of them.
We go to Bath & Body Works,
smell some more,
>sweet pea, peaches & cream.
My head spinning with smells,
when I see—

Nancy the security guard
who called the police
on my mom
that final day.

        I duck around the corner.

Tell Lauren we need to get some
pretzels and lemonade.
She says if she does she won't be hungry
for popcorn at the movie.
I tell her it's more fun that way.
                                    To be overfilled.
Have to say it quickly
                to dodge Nancy.

After pretzels,
we get out to the parking lot—
we have to walk through it
to get to the movies
the very same lot
Mom got so mad
            she lost me—
Lauren pulls
Aveda products
out of her bag.
My heart speeds up,
I lose my breath
I look around the lot for Nancy.

Tell Lauren she needs to take those back.

She says no. She's going to raise so much money
for kids like her brother—
and who needs such fancy shampoo anyway.
I say fine, hurrying Lauren
away from that bad-luck parking lot,
Nancy's evil eye.
I wanted today to be something
easy,
       happy,
   free.
But now with these shampoos,
Nancy's stare,
joy   escapes me.

Someone Like That

During the movies,
a text from a strange number:
Its mom sneaking on a hidden cell
I run out of the theater
tell me something good quick
I look around,
don't want to tell her where I am.

So, instead, I type, I've made a good friend.
Her name's Lauren and she is into . . .
shoplifting? I almost say, then write . . .
justice.
Mom types back,
says we could use someone
like that in our lives.

I love you so much

I write, but I don't hear back.
She must have had to stop.
When I return,
Lauren smiles at me,
asks me if I'm OK,
I say yes,
she says good,

a car crashes into another
as she passes the popcorn.

Yes, I Know, I Can

After the movies,
the shampoos inside her backpack.
Our knees curled up,
         back home,
         on my bed.
Carl's homemade kale chips,
at our side.
I want to tell her I felt
         anxious today.
         Want to tell her why.
But she asks about my kaleidoscope.
I say it was—is—
my mom's.
She says she'd like to know more
sometime about everything, what happened.
She doesn't want to ignore what's real.
Not anymore.
I nod.
I tell her I really like that about her.
She beams. Like I've given her a prize.
I put my hand on a chip.
Put it back down.
She tells me how she got caught
by her parents.
But she won't give up,
tells me about a girl named Hailey,

more about Jenna.
And I almost tell her about my dad.
About what my mom did on that last day.
But before I can,
she asks me
if I can help her hide the stuff
she's taking to sell.

For a minute,
I'm mad.
Wondering again
      is she using me?
      Is she just asking me
      because she has no one else?
She eats a kale chip and makes a face.
"Not quite like the real thing," she says.
I laugh.
Think of Cassidy and me
and a bag of UTZ potato chips between us.
Lauren decided to be my friend
even though I was a stranger.
She's all I have.
Think about Amy's room,
how no one is allowed to go in.
I tell her I think—
    Mr. Ellis says you need to be confident, to make a choice,
Lauren's smile, beaming eyes—
I shake my head and start again:
      "Yes—
            I know—
                  I can."

LAUREN

Easier to Breathe

The Saturday before Thanksgiving, I sat at my desk, attempting to focus on my math homework and staring out the window into Amy's dark room. That's where Sierra hid the Aveda shampoos and the cuff links Mom and Dad think are for her dad and the money they think is for the Simplicity-a-Thon.

The lights in there were off, so I couldn't see anything, but I kept picturing the tan bottles and the shiny gold cuff links under Amy's old bed. They must look so tiny under there. So insignificant. And then the too-thin envelope of cash Sierra put in Amy's closet.

I needed to figure out how to get more stuff to add to the stash under the bed and thicken up that envelope in the closet. Good stuff, like the Fitbit and the swirly ring. Stuff that's worth a lot more than a few fancy bottles of shampoo and somebody's old cuff links, even if they are real gold.

I sat there for a whole half hour, only finishing one measly word problem, until I got a notification that somebody bought the cuff links. Which was good but meant there would be even less stuff left under Amy's bed. Before I could text Sierra to see when I could pick up the cuff links, Mom came up and announced it was time to pick out a "hostess gift" for Aunt Jill and Aunt Becky since Dad and I are going to their house for Thanksgiving dinner.

I said we should go just go to one of the stores right in Chestnut Hill—the one that sells kitchen stuff, maybe, since Becky loves to cook, or the one that sells crafts from Africa and Latin America and the Middle East—places where people need the money from the vases and jewelry and dishes and other stuff people buy at the store. But things have been weird ever since Mom found all that stuff in my pajama drawer, and she's trying extra hard to make them OK. So she said we should take the train into Center City for a "girls' outing" instead.

"Let's go to Anthropologie and look at their housewares for Aunt Jill and Aunt Becky!" she told me. "And then we can go anywhere else you want on Walnut Street! Maybe we can find you some new winter clothes, now that it's getting colder! Maybe Sierra wants to join! Or Audrey—it could give you a chance to reconnect!"

She was speaking all in exclamations, and her face was all lit up, like she was so sure I'd be thrilled with her idea and so proud of herself for thinking of something I'd love. And the thing is, I *would* have been thrilled last year to go shopping, just me, Mom, and Audrey. I would have loved to have Mom to myself for a day and to try on sweaters and boots and leggings with Audrey. But Audrey and I are done, so there's no point in "reconnecting." And there's nothing wrong with the sweaters and boots and leggings I already have.

"I think Audrey and Sierra are busy," I lied.

I couldn't make myself tell Mom I wouldn't go, though—not

when her face was so lit up and I knew her smile would disappear and her shoulders would sink the second I said no.

But as soon as we got off the train at Suburban Station, I really, really wished I had. On the walk to 18th and Walnut, we passed three different people who sat on the sidewalk with cardboard signs that read HOMELESS and cups to collect money: a dirty-faced boy who only looked a few years older than Ryan, an old lady with no jacket and her hair in two braids like a little kid, and a man in a wheelchair.

It's not like I've never seen homeless people begging for money, but I guess I sort of used to tune them out. "There are charities and shelters set up to help people on the street," Dad told me once. "There's no way we can give money to every single homeless person we see, so if we want to make a difference, we can donate to those organizations."

But as Mom's shiny, highlighted hair bounced against her shoulders and her designer purse swung back and forth while we walked down 18th Street, I felt that about-to-throw-up tightness in my throat. Maybe Dad's right that giving to a charity can have a bigger impact than giving to one person, but I doubt he actually remembers to give to homelessness charities. And he *can't* be right that we shouldn't help one person just because we can't help every person. That's like saying that just because I can't get enough money to pay for OT sessions for *every* person on the spectrum, I shouldn't bother trying to pay for anybody's.

"I think we should have given money to those homeless people," I said as we walked up to Anthropologie. "Maybe we could go back?"

But Mom said, "What homeless people?" because she

hadn't even *noticed* them, and then she opened the tall, heavy door to the store and stood there with one hand on the door and the other gripping the bottom of her big designer bag, waiting for me to go in.

"I . . . I can't," I told her. "We have to go back."

She sighed. "Honey, if you come inside with me now and help me pick out something for Aunt Jill and Aunt Becky, I promise I'll stop to give money to every homeless person we pass on the way back to the train station."

"It might not be the same homeless people then!" I squeaked.

"Whoever's out then will need the money just as much," Mom said. She was using her trying-not-to-lose-it voice, which is slower and higher than her regular one.

And the tightness in my throat spread all the way down to my stomach, because she was right. Even if we went back to the people out there now *and* looked for more people on our way back to the train, there would be more people a few blocks east and a few blocks west, and we'd never even see them at all. I started to feel like maybe it wasn't anywhere near enough to give money to the people on our route back to the train station. And it might not be enough to give money to Jenna, when she's only one of thousands and thousands of OTs, and all of them probably have clients like Hailey.

Two women wearing long coats and carrying shopping bags wanted to walk out of the store, so Mom had to step behind the door to give them room.

"I'm trying to have a nice day with you, Lauren," Mom said. "Please?"

Her slow, high, fake-calm voice was rubbed worn now, like

175

the old purse she'd retired when she got this new one. A teeny-tiny part of me wanted to rewind to last year, when I would have raced into the store and hugged Mom just for agreeing to take me shopping and tuned out the homeless people on the street just like she had. But I couldn't, of course. I followed her into the store because my brain was too jumbled to do anything else.

We went downstairs to where the house decoration stuff was, and Mom stopped to ooh and aah over everything. Candlesticks, tablecloths, coffee cups, tea sets, dish towels. All these things that nobody needs at all.

I shimmied out of my jacket, but the store was way too hot, anyway.

"Look how beautiful!" Mom picked up a teapot with pastel flowers painted on.

"Aunt Jill and Aunt Becky don't like pastels," I reminded her.

I wasn't sure they'd like anything in this whole pretty, perfume-y store, actually. I tried to fan my face with one hand, but I just kept getting hotter.

Mom gave me a guilty smile. "But wouldn't it be pretty with our pastel mugs at home?"

"We barely even drink tea!" I told her, loudly enough that the lady straightening dish towels frowned at me.

Mom must have finally remembered what I'd said after they found the stuff in my pajama drawer—about how I don't like it that we don't live simply—because she nodded and put the teapot down. "You're right, honey."

She walked toward the vases and candlesticks, and I pushed up the sleeves of my sweater, but that didn't cool me down, either. So many embroidered dish towels and frilly aprons and monogrammed mugs.

"How about these?" Mom called.

She held up brightly colored potholders that might sort of match Aunt Jill and Becky's cheerful, cluttered kitchen. They have potholders already, but they're a little bit old and stained. They could buy replacements for less than half the cost of these, but everything was too hot and my throat was still too tight and we weren't going to find anything better, so I nodded.

"Maybe a candle, too," Mom added. "Do you want to choose the scent?"

We sniffed the candles in all the pretty glass jars. Cider and mulled wine and lavender. Then mint and rosemary, like the Aveda shampoos. I wanted to grab a few of those candles, slip them into the bottom of my bag where they'd clink against one another and remind me that I'm not just sitting back and pretending it doesn't matter, how screwed up everything is. That I'm trying to fix *something*, and I won't give up just because I can't fix *everything*.

After I took those shampoos when I was at the mall with Sierra, I could breathe so much easier. It was as if I'd been up on top of a mountain where the air was too thin, but then I got back to the bottom. Right away, everything felt good and bright and hopeful, the way it had when Dad replaced all the old lightbulbs in our kitchen.

I needed some of that easy-to-breathe brightness right now, but Mom was standing too close. So I pointed to the rosemary one and said, "That one smells the best. Can we go now?"

"Don't you want to look for any clothes? I know you're worried about"—she paused to look for the right words—"being too extravagant. But we could at least check the sale room. Or do you want to go straight to Urban Outfitters?"

I could probably find some more jeans or other clothes to sell, but Mom and Dad are paying too much attention now. Mom already asked me about the ones from Lucky, but I told her they were a little too big, so I was saving them for when they fit.

"Unless you're hungry for lunch?" Mom asked, and I nodded.

"I am," I lied. "I'm really, really hungry."

It only took her a few seconds to put her special-girls'-outing smile back on. "OK. Let's pay and then find something yummy!"

So we headed upstairs, and when we got to the front of the line, the cashier said, "These potholders are the cutest! Would you like these things wrapped in tissue? And would you like a gift box?"

"Yes to both, please," Mom said.

She was still smiling, and when she caught my eye, I made myself smile back, even though I couldn't stop thinking about those candles I could have sold if I'd been able to sneak them into my purse. And how many homeless people Mom and I wouldn't see on our walk back to the train station, and how many OTs there are in Philadelphia, and in Pennsylvania, and in the world.

Mom checked something on her iPhone while the cashier turned around to find the right size box and wrap our stuff in tissue paper.

There was nobody in line behind us, and nobody was looking at me, and there was a sale bin right at the end of the counter, full of sparkly hair clips and rings with giant round stones.

I reached into the bin—I could pretend I was just looking at the stuff if anyone noticed—and I pulled out three hair clips and a ring.

Mom looked up from her phone just as I slipped the stuff into my bag. "Dad wants us to bring him one of those cookies he likes, from that place on 16th."

Then the cashier turned back around. "How does this box look for you?"

Neither of them knew what I'd done. My next breath came in easily, and the whole store lit up brighter, and for the first time all day, I felt completely sure that I was doing everything I could to make things better, and as long as I kept trying, then everything might actually be OK.

Just as Mom had promised, she gave a dollar to each of the two homeless people we passed on the way back to the train. The guy in the wheelchair was there still, but the other two people were gone. There was a lady holding a scrawny orange cat on the corner where the dirty-faced boy had been.

My brain started to spin, wondering where those other people had gone and whether I should be saving my money for homeless people instead of autistic kids—or for homeless, autistic kids? But I reached into my purse and rubbed the cool, smooth, torquoise stone in the ring I'd taken until my thoughts slowed down.

Back in Mt. Airy, Mom and I walked home from the train station, and I went right to Sierra's so I could drop off the new stuff to store and pick up the cuff links.

Anne let me in, wearing a cozy off-white sweater and smiling her easy smile.

"Lauren! What a nice surprise. Sierra's upstairs working on the computer. Come on in!"

When she reached out to close the door behind me, I noticed something thin and shiny in her hand. An earring hook.

"Are you working on your jewelry?"

She used to invite me over sometimes to help her make earrings or necklaces or bracelets, and I loved to sift through beads and stones that could be combined in so many different ways to make so many different pretty things.

"I sure am. There's a craft show next weekend, after Thanksgiving. Have you heard of Small Business Saturday?"

I didn't answer, though, because I was remembering how one year, she made jewelry out of crummy old spoons. She flattened out the top part that scoops and bent the spoons into cuff bracelets, and suddenly the tarnished parts looked interesting, not just old.

Nothing says "simplicity" better than bracelets made out of crummy spoons.

"Sierra's told you about the Simplicity-a-Thon, right?" I said. "Has she told you we're looking for prizes?"

Anne's eyebrows edged together. She doesn't coat her skin with makeup the way Mom does, so I could see the faint wrinkles that lined her forehead.

"I don't believe I've heard about the prizes, no."

Sierra showed up on the stairs then, a few steps down from the top. She leaned against the railing and hooked one foot behind the other ankle, so one bent knee stuck out to the side. She was sort of frowning. Like maybe she didn't want Anne to know we needed prizes still, even though we're running out of time?

But we only had two so far, and at our last meeting, we talked about how we need one more so we can have a first-, second-, and third-place winner. It's not like I can get *my* parents to offer anything simple, but Anne's perfect. Maybe Sierra was frowning about something else.

"Tell her, Sierra," I said, but Sierra shook her head so slightly that I almost couldn't tell she'd moved.

"What are the prizes, Sierra?" Anne asked, and I recognized the way her voice sounded—like she was layering an exclamation point on top of the question mark at the end. Like maybe then her own extra enthusiasm could rub off on Sierra. Like Mom, trying so hard to connect.

"They're all supposed to be, um, activities where people can create things instead of stuff that we'd have to buy," Sierra said.

She didn't say anything else, though, so I told the rest.

"Mariah got her dad to donate a cooking lesson, and Jake's dad is giving a woodworking session."

Anne nodded slowly. "Would you like me to offer a jewelry-making lesson?"

She was looking up the stairs at Sierra, not at me. Sierra swung her bent knee forward and backward and then planted her foot flat on the step.

"OK. Thanks," she said finally. Then she turned to me. "Are you coming upstairs?"

"Yep, I'm coming. Thank you, thank you, thank you, Anne! This is going to be great!" I said, and Anne reached out to squeeze my arm.

"Thank *you*, Lauren." She smiled so big, the skin around her eyes crinkled. "It's so nice to be able to help."

And I knew exactly what she meant. It's so, so nice to be able to help.

The Simplicity-a-Thon started at the end of the day on Monday. Mariah had a guitar lesson, Gordy and Oscar had basketball, and the fifth-grade girls had to meet with their Spanish teacher, but Jake, Sierra, and I sat at the front of Mr. Ellis's room while people came in to sign up and turn in the money they'd collected from sponsors.

Sierra's job was putting each person's donations into a labeled envelope so Mr. Ellis could count up the earnings and figure out the three winners. Jake and I were in charge of having people read the no-electronics-for-twenty-four-hours pledge and sign their initials.

Max Sherman hadn't collected any donations, but he slapped a five-dollar bill onto the desk in front of Sierra.

"Sign me up, Daisy!" he told her. That's what he's called her ever since Halloween, even though I specifically told him she was a sunflower. "If I can't use a computer, then I can't do half my homework tonight!"

But even if a few other people only signed up for the same reason, almost seventy-five people entered. Even Audrey and Emma waltzed into Mr. Ellis's room, arms linked and money in hand. There was nobody reading the no-electronics pledge on my clipboard, but they waited in front of Jake's, anyway.

Audrey made a big point of calling, "Bye, Jake! Bye, Mr. Ellis!" when they left.

I caught Sierra's eye, stuck out my tongue, and made my eyes go crossed, which made her giggle.

Jake caught me doing it. "Cute," he said.

And even though he was teasing me, the word *cute* coming out of Jake's mouth set me off giggling, too, even more than Sierra.

Tuesday afternoon at 2:30, the gym was way louder than on Halloween. We were only thirty minutes away from the end of the last school day before Thanksgiving break, and almost half the middle school was thirty minutes away from turning on their cell phones for the first time in twenty-four hours, too.

Even Mr. Ellis couldn't project loudly enough for anyone to hear him, so he picked up the microphone, tapped it, and then held a hand up for silence. All the fifth and sixth graders held their hands up, too, which is what we're all supposed to do. "Hands up, mouths shut"—that's the rule. After I saw Jake's hand shoot up without any hesitation, I raised mine, too, even though most of the other seventh and eighth graders didn't.

"As you might have heard, this Thursday happens to be Thanksgiving," Mr. Ellis said, and the entire gym erupted in cheers. He put his hand up again, waiting for everybody to quiet back down before he continued. "Today, I'm feeling very, very thankful for the hardworking Worship and Ministry group and this entire community, because we have earned $4,230 that will go straight to Habitat for Humanity and their important mission!"

The applause exploded again, even louder, and across the gym, Jake pointed at me, as if this was all because of me.

Sierra leaned in to whisper, "See? You turned Thanksgiving into something good."

And, yeah, I'd only gotten $75 worth of donations total from my parents and Aunt Jill since I'd been busy trying to sell stuff for Jenna. And I sort of wished I could take at least some of that $4,000 to add to what I'd made so far for kids like Hailey. And there were all those homeless people I hadn't helped at all.

But still. I smiled my biggest smile at Jake, squeezed Sierra's hand, and cheered as loudly as I could.

Mr. Ellis announced the winners then. "First place goes to one of our Worship and Ministry leaders, Jake Paterson-Willis!"

Jake stood up, grinning, and high-fived the eighth graders who held their hands out to him as he walked up to Mr. Ellis. The collar of his light blue shirt stuck up in the back in one place instead of folding all the way over, but that just made him cuter—that one tiny detail wasn't quite right.

"Second place goes to Carly Schneider," Mr. Ellis went on. "And in third place, Audrey Lee!"

Sierra and I looked at each other as Audrey popped up and strolled to the middle of the gym, her shiny silver shoes sliding against the floor and her posture super-straight, like she'd finally listened to all her mom's scolding not to slouch. She found Sierra and me in the crowd and shot us a gloat-y, eyebrows-raised smile.

"She probably just got her dad to write a check," I whispered. "I bet she didn't do any work to find sponsors at all."

"We have three terrific prizes for our winners to choose from," Mr. Ellis said. "Mariah, come on up to tell us about the three choices, and then Jake will pick first!"

Mariah stood up and read the prize descriptions.

Pick jewelry making, Jake, I thought.

I couldn't totally see a guy choosing to make jewelry— even a guy as confident as Jake. But if he did, it would be the easiest thing in the world to go next door while he was there, maybe help him thread beads onto wire. The idea of leaning over his shoulder and encouraging him as he made a necklace or bracelet for his mom made my cheeks flame so hot, I put my hands up to cover them.

But Jake said, "I'll take the cooking lesson."

I swallowed down my disappointment and told myself to stop being so selfish. This whole Simplicity-a-Thon was about doing something good for other people, anyway.

I tried to smile as Jake high-fived Mariah and as Carly picked woodworking, but then I saw the look on Sierra's face and realized: Only one option left for Audrey.

Jewelry making lessons with Anne. At Sierra's house. Right next door to mine.

Sierra looked straight down and rubbed the palm of one hand against the shiny gym floor as Mr. Ellis gave Audrey the jewelry-making certificate. And then she barely said anything when we joined the swarm of people leaving the gym. When I asked her if she thought anybody had bought the shampoos or the Anthropologie stuff during the last twenty-four hours when I couldn't check, she only shrugged.

As soon as we made it into the hallway, I felt a hand on my shoulder, and when I turned around, there was Jake, the back of his collar still sticking up.

Adrenaline jolted through my whole body. "Hey, congrats!" I said.

"What are you doing the Saturday after Thanksgiving break?" he asked.

I was so surprised by his question that I forgot to keep walking, and somebody ran into me from behind.

"Um, nothing, I don't think."

"Any chance you want to join me for my cooking lesson at Mariah's, then? She said her dad doesn't mind if it's two people instead of one."

I nodded, because I couldn't make my mouth say words.

"Awesome!" Then he turned on his phone and had me add my number. "You deserve a prize, too, since the whole thing was your idea. I'll text you to make a plan."

After he walked away, I pulled Sierra to the edge of the hallway.

"Did that actually just happen?"

I kept running through the interaction in my head to figure it out. Maybe he just felt bad that I didn't win anything?

"He asked you out," Sierra said. "I'm not surprised."

Asked me out. Was that really what he'd done?

We walked down the hallway to get our stuff, and Mariah waved when we passed her outside Mr. Ellis's room. We both waved back, but there was a strange look on Sierra's face. And when we finally got to our space outside Ms. Meadows's room, I picked up my backpack, but Sierra just stood there watching me.

"What is it?" I asked. "What's wrong?"

"I'm happy for you, Lauren. About Jake," she said. Then she took in a giant breath. "Just . . . please don't take anything from Mariah's house, OK?"

SIERRA

Shaky

I was so nervous
to ask Lauren
not to take anything from
Mariah's.
But Mariah has been nice
to me, too.
And she's in our group
with us.
Cares about the same things
we do.
Lauren's eyes didn't look
mad exactly
but I did feel
sick after
like I had made things
worse.

When I got home,
I looked into my kaleidoscope
and this time shook and shook

for green to
rise up
not for Mom,

for Lauren.

Every Shiny Thing

When Mom's days faded from
green to orange,
there was this in-between time—
when I could joke or snuggle her out
of her coming anger.
Like how you see storm clouds
but then the weather shifts,
the sun pushes them out
all it does is drizzle.
Now, searching for green
I wonder,
though,
if Lauren's already so gone.
Thunder—
          lightning—
                    orange.

I wonder if no warning
or joke or anything
can distract her
from stealing
then selling
every shiny thing.

Careful

I leave the kaleidoscope,
go back downstairs.
Anne's cleaning the good china,
gold-edged with birds,
for Thanksgiving.
Her brown arms lit up
by the kitchen window sun.
She asks if I can help her.
I do, careful
not to break the platter
she hands me.
A little honored
she trusts me with it.
I wonder
      what I've done
           to deserve it.

In Half

Anne says her cousin Benny
is coming and his teenage son, Leo,
they're bringing the sweet potatoes.
She says when she and Carl
got married, her cousin Benny
stood by her side
her parents so angry
she was marrying someone white.
Her parents, long since passed,
never really accepted Carl.

It reminds me of Nan
how she never liked it when Mom
had boyfriends who weren't white.
How they'd fight.

Then Anne says the caseworker called.
She's coming Saturday to take me
to visit Dad. "She also says
there's been a new development with your mom.
Maude said she has some better news to share.
She wants to do it in person."

When she says it, I drop
one of her plates,
by accident.

Tears prick my eyes
as I stare at its gold edges,
colorful birds,
now broken
in half.

Repurposed

Anne puts an arm around me
      says sometimes broken things
      get repurposed
to make something beautiful.
She takes me to the basement.
Gives me a hammer.
Tells me to smash the rest of it.
When I look at her confused
she laughs, says
      broken things
make the best jewelry.
So I take the hammer.
From birds we make
beak, foot, wing.

Hiding

Anne's being so nice to me
I feel guilty
when I sneak into Amy's room.
I sift through Lauren's box,
under Amy's bed.
Wishing I could make it vanish.
I wonder if Anne
would actually understand
Lauren's plan
and if —
or how—
I would ever feel brave
enough
to tell her.
Suddenly wish I had Lauren's
8 Ball.
Maybe it could
give me
a sign.

Almost Every Moment

The house smells of turkey.
Anne has me peeling the white potatoes.
It is hard for me to focus, wondering
almost every moment
what Maude has to say about Mom.
Suddenly, the phone's ring—
      loud as a siren—
            sends me shivers.
I can tell from Anne's voice

it's her.

Safe?

"Hi, baby girl,"
she says.
Tears slide down my face
just hearing her voice.
She says Happy Thanksgiving,
how she misses my face.
Asks what it's like where I am,
how's school.
How's Lauren, "justice girl" she calls her.
I tell her none of it is horrible
but I need her to get better,
how much I miss her.
She tells me she's trying really hard
that it won't be long, not to worry
but then I hear a man's voice in the background
and she says she has to go,
and I feel a part of me sink
as I hang up the phone.

The Only Color

Anne follows me
as I run from the phone
to my room.

                                    I ignore her
as I watch the colors in the kaleidoscope
swirl and blend and fade into one another.
I ask for green,
like a prayer,
beg for it
to rise to the top.

But when I look in again,
all I can see are mirrors.

Mom chose that man
over me.
She never gets to talk to me
but she chose him.
The colors come in, swirling:
Orange rises to the top.

Reverse

Benny and Leo arrive right on time.
Leo's tall with dark brown skin,
he reaches out his hand to shake mine.
I shake it, blushing.
Benny says we should play a game
while the grown-ups "catch up."

Leo and I both shrug.
Neither of us want to say
which game we will play.
But finally I suggest Uno,
something Dad and I played a lot
before.

Leo's so quiet
        I am the one who has to make conversation.
        I ask him about school, sports, where he lives.
He gives me one-word answers, doesn't ask me anything
just tells me to draw four.
In a last attempt,
I ask him about his mom,
he says she's not around.
Never was, so much.
He says Anne's the closest to a mom that he has.
He says he calls her every week to check in with her.

"Don't take her for granted,"

he says,
glaring at me.
I wonder how much she's told him.
How much she's told Benny.

Shocked by his words, though,
I don't ask.
He plays his card.

Reverses the turn back to me.

Not at All

During the meal,
Benny leads the conversation.
Leo and I both
still quiet.
Benny's starting a food bank.
He says it is a lot of hard work
and he is scared of being in over his head,
running a nonprofit is no joke.
Carl laughs, says tell me about it.
Talks for a while about life at the co-op.

I think about how Nan
used to shop at food banks
but Mom refused to,
even when we hardly had any money.
Instead, she would get guys in bars
to buy our groceries.

I look down at all my
turkey,
mashed potatoes,
gravy
thinking of Leo's stare
suddenly not feeling like eating
at all.

More Stares

Saturday comes,
Maude arrives.
Asks if I'm excited to see my father.
It is hard to tell, all I can really feel
is anxiety, wanting to know what's up with Mom.

She says she wants Anne and Carl there
when she tells me.
I sit on the oversized old couch by myself.
Three adults, in chairs,
staring at me.
Maude says she has good news.

    Mom's jail sentence ended up being a bit longer than
        expected.
    She had some emotional issues.
    But, after an evaluation ordered by the judge,
    they decided she was a candidate
    for "alcohol addiction rehabilitation."
    A requirement for her to get me back.
    After rehab, she will need to find a job and housing
    and then plan A is me returning home.

When Mom called me she wasn't in jail anymore.
That must have been an orderly's voice on the phone!
Someone told her time was up!

I almost jump up, I'm so excited.
But I can tell from Carl's look to Anne
that they are only pretending to smile.

Faking it till they make it.

Ride

When we get to the prison
to see him
they tell us
he's been in a fight
was sent to solitary, sorry.
Maude gets so angry
says she called just yesterday
the guard shrugs
says
things can change
so fast. Blink of an eye.

On the way back
to Anne and Carl's,
Maude asks me why I'm not
more upset.
I tell her if you ride a roller coaster enough
it starts to feel like a carousel.
All the up, downs make a circle,
spinning.

Beside, Between

Before Maude leaves,
I ask when I can see Mom.

She says she will talk to Mom's counselor
and get back to me.

It used to be just Mom and me
snuggling,
under blankets,
watching TV

now there is so much space

and so many people

between us.

Half-Made

When we get home,
    back too early,
    Audrey's there.
Working with Anne.
Making jewelry.
Anne waves me over,
asks me to join them.
She turns up her Joni Mitchell.
Makes some more tea.
I think about Dad
all alone now
in a cell.
No music.
Nothing.
Wonder what Mom's allowed in rehab.
Anne makes sure not to ask about Dad
in front of Audrey.

Audrey keeps cursing
as she tries to bend wire
around and through beads.
She keeps dropping the cutters.

And looking over at me
       as I put wire through bead, carefully.
                              I decide it is for Mom,
                as I braid wire
       pull it through
green glass.
Audrey has to keep asking Anne questions.
Anne touches her shoulder,
teaches her the same thing a few times,
always speaks gently.
At the end,
       Audrey is so excited about her new earrings and
              necklace.
       Though a lot of the wire is crooked and some beads
              are loose.
Says she hasn't made anything this crafty
maybe ever.
She laughs.

I look away as she and Anne hug.

Go up to my room,
leaving my own half-made bracelet on the table.

Into the Mirror

Sunday, I ask Carl
if we could pick up Cassidy . . .
figure he'll ask fewer questions than Anne.

On the way, he asks if I've ever heard of
companion gardening.
He laughs at the way I say, "Um, no."
He says one of the most exciting organic gardening tricks
he's learned in recent years
is that some plants do better in proximity to each other.
He's explaining how they help each other
grow safer,
stronger
as we pull up to Cassidy's.
      Lena on the peeling porch smoking.
      The twins running around the front yard.
      No winter jackets.
I look at Carl and wonder what he's thinking.
But he only grins.
      I look down at the Northwest Friends sweatshirt
      wish I hadn't worn it.
Carl marches out of the car, up to the house,
extends his hand to Lena.
Lena gives me a big hug. Says she can't wait till I come back.

Cassidy looks surprised when she sees Carl.
Probably because he's so much older than our moms.
Not what she expected.

In the old car,
Cassidy and I sit in the back together.
Cassidy chomps her gum.
She talks fast, nervous, tells me
about all our old friends.
I worry Carl is going to finish his lesson
on companion gardening.
Instead—
he just smiles in the rearview mirror.
I can tell he's not smiling for himself
it's for Cassidy,
it's for me.

Spells

Cassidy surprises me, says she loves all this stone.
Reminds her of Harry Potter.
She casts spells in the foyer.

We run up to my room,
and Seeger follows us.
She asks to go into Amy's room,
but I tell her we can't.
Lie and say it's Carl's office,
figure it isn't my secret to tell her.
And don't want to risk her seeing Lauren's stuff.
What would she think of Lauren stealing for kids with
    special needs?
Would she laugh? Think it was a waste?
I think about introducing them
but—now that it's a possibility, I worry—
        Would Cassidy think Lauren's stuck-up?
        Would Lauren think Cassidy was hyper?

"I know you say you're not lucky.
But I would love this much space
away from my sisters," she says.

"Maybe you think you would,
but if it happened, you wouldn't."

"Sierra, you have a whole bathroom to yourself?!"

Am I supposed to feel guilty?

Cassidy blows a bubble.
Then snaps it.
"What's that?" Cassidy points out the window.

"Compost.
They're big into the environment.
They use that dirt made from food
to help grow other food."

"Why don't they just go to the store? They're rich."
I think of Lauren.
I shrug.
"The rich people out here don't seem that into being rich."

"That's weird," Cassidy says.
"If I was rich, I'd shop till I dropped."

"I know what you mean," I say simply.
Though as I say it, I'm not sure.

"Little orphan Annie, can I please run away and stay here
    with you?"
She puts her hands in a begging position and bats her eyes.

My heart burns wanting to yell at her,
how could she say she wants to be torn from her family?

Can't she see how hard this is for me?

Can't she see this isn't a joke?

But instead, I do what Cassidy and I always do:
ignore stuff.

We stop talking and play cards
        we slap jack after jack
                until our hands burn red.

All Because

This time,
       Mom calls
               and it is easy
                      to talk to her
                              her voice
                              sounds clear
                              like a sunny-day
                              ocean
                                      and I tell her
                                      I saw Cassidy
                                      and I tell her
                                      about Lauren
                                      and the club
                                      and Seeger
       and she says I sound
       happy
    and I say it's all because
    of rehab,
all because of her.
And my earlier anger at Cassidy falls away.

A Little Away

Back at school,
>   Lauren asks why I didn't come over
>   this weekend.
Tell her I was really busy,
tell her I got some good news about my mom.
But I don't say what
and I don't tell her about making jewelry with Audrey.
Or not introducing her to Cassidy.
It would just upset her.
And I can't do that.
Without her other friends,
>   I am the only one
>   to help make her happy.
She tells me she has more stuff she needs to hide
and quickly, she says.
Asks if she can come by later.
I ask her what kind of stuff.
She says,
"Things nobody needs.
A sweater,
a dress.
Some shoes."
Not wanting her to get in trouble,
knowing this is what she needs from a friend,
I shrug, say fine.

During Worship & Ministry,
we talk about our next event.
It will be like Secret Santa
  but people will do favors
  for others
  instead of giving gifts.
  Like Mom and I used to do.
Lauren and Jake sit even closer together
than they did last week.

Wonder what Jake would think of Lauren's plan.
I slide a little away from her.

Tell Mariah I like her jacket,
jean with small holes all over it.
She smiles, mouth full of braces,
says she likes mine, too.

LAUREN

The Best Person I Know

Sierra's been acting strange ever since we got back to school. A little distant. She says something's up with her mom, and she acted like it was a good something, but if it's really a good something, then I don't know why she won't tell me what it is. And I'm not sure if I'm supposed to ask about it or not or if it's unfair that I want her to ask about *my* Thanksgiving and *my* mom going to North Carolina to see Ryan without us, when my mom was only gone for four and a half days and who knows when she'll get to see her mom again.

Actually, I sort of am sure. It's definitely unfair for me to want her to ask about that, even though it felt so good to talk to her about Ryan before.

Since I can't really tell Sierra, I haven't told anybody about how Ryan sent me a new video, which was nice, except that after he wished me a Happy Thanksgiving and told me he missed me and loved me, he held up a big book of piano music and said, "Mom said you'd like to see how I can hear how a song sounds by the way the notes look on the page."

And then he played the beginning of a Beethoven sonata, glancing up at the sheet music every few seconds and stumbling over a couple of notes, even though he'd be able to play the song perfectly if he just listened to it on YouTube and then copied the sounds.

"My teacher says I'm one of the fastest learners he's ever worked with," Ry said once he stopped playing.

But I don't understand why he has to learn to read music to begin with. He *hated* it when he took piano lessons when he was in fifth grade, and the teacher tried to teach him to follow the notes and rests and beats. And Jenna specifically said we should be honoring his strengths. Why would these supposed experts at Piedmont think it's a good idea to force him to play someone else's way instead of *his* way?

I also haven't told anybody about how Mom came back Sunday night with a strange, smushed, bakery-made pie and a too-wide smile stretched across her face.

"It's a lemon pie with meringue on top and a salty cracker crust!" she said. "A North Carolina delicacy."

There were still a few slices of Aunt Jill and Aunt Becky's homemade cherry in the fridge, but Dad took out plates and silverware and served up Mom's weird pie while Mom showed me photos on her phone. Picture after picture of the food at the Piedmont Thanksgiving. One of Ryan standing behind a giant bowl of salad and one of him pointing to an untouched mound of vegetables on his plate. I enlarged them to see if he was smiling his real smile or not, but they were too out of focus to tell.

"Ryan and the others picked the kale and beets for this salad and the broccoli and cauliflower for this side dish. Don't they look great?"

"I guess," I said, and, I mean, they looked fine, but not like anything Ryan would actually want to put into his mouth.

I shoveled down a bite of the tangy, slightly soggy pie and wished it were cherry instead.

Dad was already finishing the crust of his piece, but Mom hadn't touched the "tiny sliver" she'd told him to cut for her.

"And all the students used these special name tags for the meal," Mom said, scrolling to a photo of three laminated rectangles that each said RYAN—one green, one yellow, and one red. "If they had the green tag on, that meant they were open to social interactions. Yellow meant they wanted to talk but might not have the energy to start conversations, so you should engage them. And red meant they needed some time to themselves. Isn't that a great idea?"

"That's wonderful," Dad said, helping himself to a bite of Mom's pie. "What a smart way to make it easier for Ryan to ask for what he needs, huh, Laur?"

"Well, did he do it?" I asked.

Mom blinked, and I surprised myself, too, a little, with how sharp my voice sounded.

"I just mean . . . did he ever switch the tag to red to tell you he needed a break?"

"No," Mom admitted, but then she went back to her extra cheerful voice. "But I think he was happy to be social for almost the whole time, really."

Almost the whole time. Which meant that at least once, everything had gotten to be too much for him. So this super-amazing color-coded name-tag system isn't such a miracle after all.

Mom blinked a few more times. There were tears in her eyes, even though supposedly everything at Piedmont was just so wonderful.

"He's doing so well, Laur," she said. "He's so excited about everything he's learning. He seemed so much more at home than when we went for Family Weekend."

But how am I supposed to believe that everything's suddenly better when they wouldn't let me see it for myself? And when they thought the Keller School was a good place, too, for a while there?

Mom got up and started sorting through the pile of mail that Dad had left out on the counter.

"Oh, good. The invitation for the Lees' holiday party came!" she said, holding up a gold-rimmed invitation.

"I hope they have those pistachio cookies again," Dad said.

I pushed away my half-eaten weird North Carolina pie as I thought of last year's party, when Ryan played Christmas carols on the piano and Audrey and I were still best friends.

"You want to go, don't you, Lauren?" Mom asked.

She thinks things are better with Audrey and me now because I had to use "going to Audrey's" as my excuse when I mailed the cuff links from the post office.

"Uh, sure," I said.

When I excused myself to finish my homework and picked up my phone, there was a new message waiting for me.

I just invented the greatest leftover sandwich of all time. Cranberry sauce, stuffing, creamy green beans, & turkey, all heated up till the cranberry oozes out.

From Jake. He'd texted on Thanksgiving Day, too, but only to say Happy Thanksgiving.

I read the sandwich text three times before I thought of a good enough reply.

You'd better patent that ASAP!

Then I added a thumbs-up emoji and a smiley face. Because for the first time in that whole long, messed-up holiday weekend, I was grinning.

I figured I'd tell Sierra about the text as soon as I saw her the next morning. But things have felt so off that I haven't told her about that, either.

The next Saturday afternoon, I sat on our front steps, shivering while I waited for Jake.

I had almost asked Sierra to come over and help me decide whether to wear my dark green flannel button-down or my soft, light blue sweater. Last year, Audrey and I had strategized about what to wear just to walk to Starbucks when there was a chance we might run into guys from our grade. But Jake's not the kind of guy who cares what a girl is wearing, and I'm trying not to care about that kind of thing anymore, either.

While I waited, though, I kept wishing that Sierra would happen to come out, pulling Seeger's leash, or see me and want to keep me company. But she didn't.

Maybe even though she made it sound like something good had happened with her mom, it was really something bad that she didn't want to talk about yet. Or maybe I said something wrong again—like when I thought we should give the Simplicity-a-Thon money to foster kids—but I have no idea what.

Finally, Jake's mom pulled up in a little silver car that was old like Anne and Carl's, and I hoped Jake couldn't tell that the shiny new SUVs out front were my parents'.

Jake opened up the passenger-side door, and I heard his

mom say, "Are you sure Mariah's house isn't too far? I can drop you both off there."

But Jake shook his head and said thanks anyway, and then his mom called, "Hi, Lauren!" even though she's never actually met me. I didn't know if she was the Paterson part of Jake's last name or the Willis part or both, so I couldn't call her by name back, but I smiled and waved.

"Call me when you want me to pick you up, sweetie!" she called to Jake, and even though the air was super-cold, my cheeks heated up.

Jake's mom calls him "sweetie." I loved knowing that so much, I had to bite the inside of my cheek. For a split second, I pictured telling Audrey, but of course I can't now.

"You lead the way!" Jake told me.

I'm the one who'd told him Mariah's house was within walking distance, but his jacket wasn't as puffy as mine, and he wasn't wearing a hat or gloves. As we started out toward Mariah's, I hoped he wasn't freezing.

"You'd better be hungry, because I got to pick the menu, and we're making the best meal ever," he said as we turned off our street. He sounded too cheerful to be freezing, at least.

"As good as your patented leftovers sandwich?" I asked, and he laughed.

He took his hand out of his jacket pocket, and for a second I thought he might reach out to grab mine.

Instead, he wrapped one finger around another. "Fingers crossed."

I held up my gloved hand and crossed my fingers, too.

I wasn't worried about the meal we were making but crossed my fingers that Sierra wasn't mad at me and that everything was OK with her mom and that the cashmere sweater Aunt Jill gave me on Thanksgiving because it didn't fit her and the Anthropologie hair clips would sell soon.

We were making pigs in blankets for appetizers, gourmet mac and cheese for the meal, and Black Forest cake, which is chocolate with whipped cream and cherries, for dessert. All of Jake's favorite things, plus a roasted broccoli and cauliflower side dish that Mariah's dad added so we'd have something healthy on the menu. It made me think of the one at Ryan's school that Mom had taken a picture of.

Mariah's house is smaller than mine, but you can tell how much her dad likes to cook because her kitchen is way bigger than ours, and everything in it looks brand-new. I was wondering how much the fancy sandwich press on the counter would sell for if I could somehow sneak it out, when I remembered how Sierra's forehead had wrinkled up when she told me not to take anything.

Mariah's dad introduced himself as Mr. Freedman and said, "I have all the ingredients ready! Just pick an apron, and we'll start."

Her other dad, who said to call him Jonathan, didn't stick around for very long. "I like to stay away when the magic's happening in here," he told us. "Safer this way, so I can't mess anything up."

"Like when you accidentally added curry powder instead of ginger to that pumpkin bread?" Mariah's little sister called from the living room.

"Curry and ginger are very close to the same color," he said, laughing. "It could have happened to anyone!"

Then he hurried off to the living room, and Mr. Freedman pointed to the aprons hanging on a special rack near the oven. One of them was pink and flowery and frilly, and it looked like something you could buy for more than fifty bucks at Anthropologie, except that the bottom was stained. I chose a red-and-white striped one with a smiling lobster on the front, and Jake picked bright green gingham and asked me to tie it in the back for him.

Mariah peeked into the kitchen to say hi, and Jake turned around to face her even though I hadn't finished tying the bow to hold his apron closed.

"Aren't you going to help?" he asked, and Mariah messed with her fading bangs as she shrugged.

"I guess if you want me to?"

"The more the merrier. Right, Lauren?"

I wanted to shake my head and say, *I thought you wanted to hang out with me! You texted me about a sandwich!*

But I made myself smile at Mariah. "Definitely!"

"I'm not wearing that awful pink apron, though," Mariah warned her dad.

I remembered something Mariah had said one time before Worship and Ministry, about how one of her dads is always buying her girly things that aren't her style at all. I was pretty sure I could guess which dad.

I was about to offer to trade, but Mariah's dad took off his plain white one and handed it to Mariah. "Fine. I'll wear it."

He did a little twirl once he'd put it on, and Jake applauded.

And even though I wasn't so sure anymore that Sierra was right and Jake had asked me *out*-out, it was pretty fun, making all that food. We sang along to Christmas songs, and Mariah's dad kept complimenting my attention to detail, and Jake shouted like a little kid when the cream he was whipping finally started to get thick and airy enough for the cake.

But then when I was helping to ice the cake, I dripped a little bit of cherry sauce on the top of my sweater, just above where the apron hit.

"It's just a sweater. It's not important," I said, but Mariah's dad sent me upstairs to wash it with soap in Mariah and her sister's bathroom, since Jake was using the one downstairs.

I scrubbed and scrubbed the spot until the dark red stain faded, but I used so much water that the whole front of the sweater ended up soaked.

I searched under the sink for a hair dryer, and there, in front of a wall of extra toilet paper, was a sealed pink box with fancy perfume inside. The price tag was stuck to the bottom: $78. For perfume! Mr. Freedman had probably bought it to turn Mariah into somebody girly.

Please don't take anything from Mariah's house, Sierra had told me.

But when I started thinking about Hailey with her puffy ponytail, getting so upset during that Jenga game, there wasn't any room left in my brain to keep remembering Sierra's wrinkled-up forehead and worried brown eyes.

Yes, I wasn't planning on taking anything, but Mariah didn't even want this perfume. Why let it just sit here when I could do something good by selling it?

But then what if Mariah or Mr. Freedman noticed, and

they figured out what I'd done? What if Mariah told Sierra or, even worse, Jake?

I found the hair dryer and took it out, put the perfume back where I'd found it, and closed the cabinet door.

Forget it, I told myself as I tried to dry the front of my sweater. *You can find something else to take tomorrow.*

But now that I knew it was right there, expensive and unopened, my hands were all shaky and I couldn't breathe right and I didn't care about the wet spot on my sweater and I knew it for a fact: I'd never be able to go back downstairs and ice the cake as if everything was normal unless I took the perfume.

So I opened the cabinet back up, slid the box into the apron pocket, and then moved it into my jacket pocket once I got back downstairs.

It was dark and even colder outside after we ate all the food we'd made. Jake and I stepped out the front door with a big bag of leftovers.

"If you're not warm enough, we can call my mom to pick us up here." He shifted the leftover bag so he could put his bare hands into his pockets, and then he took a little step closer to me. "I just like the idea of telling her to come to your house and walking back there, 'cause then it's only you and me for a little while."

My heart started pounding so hard, he must have been able to hear it. He was only standing a foot or two away. I wasn't quite brave enough to look up at him, but I smiled.

"I like that idea, too," I said.

So we walked and shivered, and Jake asked me about my favorite foods. "What would you have wanted us to make today if you were the one choosing?"

"I like mac and cheese like you," I said, but then I couldn't think of any other foods right away.

Mashed potatoes. Chicken fingers. Vanilla cake with white icing. Those are the foods I asked for on my last birthday, but those are Ryan's favorites, really. He's not going to be around for my thirteenth birthday in May. What foods will I ask for then?

"Well, one time I had this asparagus and ricotta ravioli with pesto sauce at my aunt's," I said. "She was afraid it would be too grown-up for me, but I loved it. I was sort of proud of myself, actually. For having mature taste."

Jake smiled. "Very sophisticated."

I put my hands into my coat pockets and was surprised when my fingers hit the perfume box, because I'd forgotten it was there. The other weekend at Anthropologie, I'd felt so much better when I reached into my purse and rubbed my fingers over the smooth stone of the ring I'd taken and the scratchy square jewels on the hair clips. But now, the stiff cardboard sides of the box made my stomach sink. I took my hands out of my pockets, fast.

Neither of us said anything for a while as we kept walking. It was my turn to ask him something. Last year when Audrey liked Max Sherman and she met up with him to work on a science project, we planned questions she could ask him in case the conversation turned awkward. But I couldn't remember any of those questions now.

"If you could have any one superpower, what would it be?" I finally asked.

Ryan likes superheroes, so it's one of the go-to conversation starters he brainstormed with Jenna.

"Flying," Jake said without any hesitation. He didn't even act like I'd just said anything surprising, so maybe all boys like thinking about superpowers, not just Ry. "You?"

I took in a big breath and let it out in a cloud of air. When Ryan used to ask me, I'd say being invisible or reading people's minds. One time I told him I'd want the power to blink at my computer and have my English paper finish itself, but Ryan said that wasn't a real superpower.

"I wish I had the power to make the world less messed up. So everything isn't so unfair. Like, to make it so people who already have more than their share of everything would get zapped if they tried to buy more fancy stuff they didn't need or something."

Ryan might say that's not a real superpower, either.

Jake laughed, but by the time he talked, his voice sounded serious. "I think you kind of have that power already. I mean, not the zapping part maybe, but the part about making the world less messed up. Just look at the Simplicity-a-Thon. All those people raised money for a good cause because of you."

I shrugged and felt my cheeks go warm again. "Not *just* because of me."

"Mostly," Jake said. "You just . . . you care about stuff that matters. You're the best person I know."

He stopped where he was, and I kept walking, so he reached out and held on to my arm gently, right below the elbow, so I'd stop, too.

He was looking right at me, and his face is so, so cute, and his eyes are so, so kind, and he was smiling just a tiny bit—a private, just-for-me smile. His ears weren't covered, and they must have been freezing, and I wanted to put my hands over them to warm them up.

But then I shifted my weight, and the edge of the perfume box dug into my hip. Suddenly, I could only think of how disappointed in me Sierra would be if she knew I'd taken it. How upset Mariah's dad would be if he asked Mariah to wear the perfume for a special occasion and found out it was gone.

And if Jake knew what I'd done—what I couldn't stop myself from doing—would he understand that I was only trying to help? Would he still think I'm the best person he knows?

"Lauren?" Jake said.

"It's so cold," I told him, jumping up and down a little. "We should keep walking."

"OK, sure. Right. Let's go."

I couldn't look at him while we walked, though. I didn't want to see his just-for-me smile fade and his kind brown eyes switch from happy to confused.

After Jake's mom picked him up, I knocked on Sierra's door, even though I knew she might be mad at me already and what I had to tell her would make her madder. Carl told me she was in her room and to go on up, and by the time I'd climbed up the stairs and stood in her doorway, my tears were spilling out.

Sierra was lying facedown on her bed, leaning on her

elbows and reading our English book. When she saw me, she jumped up.

"What is it?" she said. "Lauren, what's wrong?"

I pulled the perfume box out of my pocket. "I didn't mean to take it. But Mariah will never use it, and I just . . . I couldn't help it, Sierra. I'm sorry."

Sierra closed her door, hugged me, and then pulled me over to the bed.

"You could give it back to Mariah on Monday," she said. "You could say . . . I don't know. We could come up with something. Some explanation."

She didn't sound mad. And she *did* hug me. But I couldn't do what she was telling me to.

"There's no way to explain it," I said. "We should just add it to the other stuff I've taken. We have to just sell it now."

Sierra's forehead wrinkled up, and she pressed her lips together.

"I'm getting kind of worried." She said it so softly, I almost couldn't hear her, and something in me shifted.

"Maybe if we can get to a thousand dollars, we can stop," I said.

That was a good number, $1,000. Maybe that was enough for ten sessions for someone like Hailey, and ten sessions could do a lot. I could feel like I'd done something meaningful if I made it to $1,000, and then Sierra and I could go back to normal.

"Are we close to a thousand dollars?" Sierra asked, and I nodded.

This was feeling better and better, having a definite

number goal to get to. "We're more than halfway there. If I get a few more really good things, we could do it before New Year's, maybe. And then we could deliver it all to Jenna, and that would be it."

"I guess," Sierra said.

I held out the perfume bottle. "Will you hide this with the rest of the stuff?"

She blew air straight up, and it made the front pieces of her blond hair float above her head for just a second.

"Please, Sierra. I don't know what else to do."

She nodded, just once. "But you'll stop by New Year's? So, less than one more month?"

"By New Year's. Definitely. As long as we've gotten a thousand dollars."

Anne called Sierra down to dinner, and I headed back home.

After I listed the perfume online, I clicked over to the part of the website where people post about things they're looking for.

Most of the listings were for big stuff I couldn't get. TVs and couches and dining room chairs. But a few were for jewelry—a rose gold chain to match a pendant, a vintage Art Deco engagement ring.

And then I saw it. A post from a guy who was looking for a holiday gift for his girlfriend. She'd lost her favorite bracelet, he said, and he wanted to replace it, but the designer didn't make the style anymore. He'd pay $300 if someone had a bracelet like it that was in good condition.

He'd posted a photo, zoomed in to show the bracelet on

a girl's hand. Swirly silver, like Mom's ring, but with big blue stones instead of a honey-colored one.

I thought of the gold-rimmed invitation Mom had stuck to our fridge, and Audrey's mom's giant jewelry collection. Audrey and I used to raid it and then take glamorous pictures of ourselves wearing fancy necklaces and bracelets and hair clips.

Three hundred dollars would get us almost all the way to one thousand. And I knew just where I could get the bracelet this guy was looking for.

SIERRA

From the Looks of It

I try to work on my history essay,
      try to think through a thesis
      make ideas fall into place
            like the settling colors of a kaleidoscope,
but all I can think about now is Mom's sober self.
The one who would listen to every detail of my day,
the one who would buy me too many school supplies.
My eye wanders to a paper on top of a stack.
A thank-you for a donation
to the Children's Hospital of Philadelphia's Cancer Center.
In Amy's name.

She died of cancer.
      Not an accident.
      Not something anyone could have prevented.

They probably did everything they could
to save her,
but it didn't matter.

A framed picture of her looks down on me.
Pale brown skin,
glasses,
tight curls,
full smile.

Go back to my essay
but think of Amy,
so young and sick,
I'm not sure
what it is
I want to say.

My ideas are colors,

                         floating,

              nothing

     stays   still, in place.

     Nothing

               falls

     into   a pattern.

A Part of Me

Carl walks in
    the donation paper still in my hand.
I tell him sorry.
He says he will tell me
    all about Amy if I want to know.
A part of me does,
    but another part of me still doesn't.
I tell him no, that's OK.
Look back to the computer.
Think of him telling me about the garden, compost.
How he seems to like to teach.
                    Ask him instead—
        my colors, swirling—
                    for help
with my essay.

Open / Shut

Carl stays up with me
way past my bedtime
and we finish an outline.
In the end, he had me find the proof
before the statement.
               A new way to think.
He walks me to my room,
Seeger wagging his tail behind,
says that was actually fun.
I laugh and say
he needs to get out more.
He pats me on the head,
opens his mouth
but then shuts it again.
I open the door.
I mean to say thank you
when I say good night.

Sleeping Garden

Before bed,
I look out the window,
at the sleeping garden, quiet
waiting to bloom
under
the
moon
light's
glow.

The Same

The next day Anne says
she knows I know
about Amy's cancer.
She says, after Amy died,
she was a mess.
Amy was so young, just eight.
It was so unfair.
      She just wanted to forget her. The pain.
      She left the house as much as she could.
But on one trip to New Orleans
on a tour
they went to an old graveyard.
She didn't want to go in,
she stood with her hands on the gates.
But through them she could read
something inscribed on one tombstone.

It read:
      Just because a person is dead
      doesn't mean that they weren't—
      beaming, fully—alive.
And she made a pact with herself,
to keep, to remember, to hold
to come back home.

I almost reach out for her hand then, but—

She hands me a pamphlet:
AlaTeen.
Says it's for kids
like me.
"Foster kids?"
I ask.
She says no, half smiles.

"It's for kids with moms like yours.
Parents with addictions."

How could other teens help me help Mom?
It makes no sense.
Besides,
my mom isn't just someone who drinks,
she's someone who loves
the beach,
kaleidoscopes,
fun houses.
She's the one who believed in me the most.

     "No one has a mom like mine,"
I whisper.

"Their experiences don't have to be exactly like yours,"
she says,
      "to feel the same."

            She tries to look at me
            but I don't want to look back
            instead I hang on to
            a picture of Mom and me in the ocean,
            riding the same wave together,

            all the way to shore.

Hiding

When I go upstairs,
I stop by Lauren's things
in Amy's room
and know I can't keep her secret
much longer.

> Now that I know that Amy was sick,
> and the room is a way to keep her alive,
> not in a creepy way
> in a way of celebration,
> it feels even worse
> hiding stolen things in there.

I take it all out
              then—
think of Lauren saying
only a month more.
Think of how Lauren's lost someone, too.
                Pack it all back.
One
by
one.

Surprise

After school
two voice messages:
        one from Cassidy
        singing me her new favorite song.

        I delete it.
        Then feel guilty.
Then,

        Anne, who says
        she, Maude, & I are going to visit Mom
        for family time at the rehab.

My stomach cartwheels.
I'm going to see Mom!

Maude and Anne pick me up.

The rehab is closer to where we used to live.
The place looks like a hospital.
Think of how much Mom hated visiting Nan there.

Mom looks small
but her eyes look clear.
And so pretty.

I break from Anne and Maude.
And run to her.

Mom and I don't let go of each other's hands.
We have to participate in a group.
All the patients and their families.
I wonder why Anne stays.

Each patient has to apologize to their families, "make amends."
       Mom says, "So sorry, baby. This will be it. I will get
           better."
       And then she looks sad when she says, "You look so
           grown up."
       And then, "Sometimes I miss you being young."
I squeeze her hand harder,

I want to tell her I still need her.

But then, Mom turns to Anne, I can tell it is so hard for her,
       but the counselor looks at her
       and she does it, says,
       "Thank you for taking care of my kid."
And even though I know I am the child and she is the
    parent,
at that moment I feel proud.

Wide-Eyed

Maude says Mom
will be released soon.
She's done great.
They think she's ready
to get a job, a house.
I wonder where she will stay when she gets out?
Lena's?

I text Cassidy
a wide-eyed, surprised emoticon
next to it, the words:
I saw Mom!!!

She texts back a smiling cat
with heart eyes.

I think how Lauren
would probably say
something more meaningful back.
Shoot a thumbs-up in response to her cat.
As we wind back down Germantown Ave.,
back to Anne and Carl's,
think of Mom's clear eyes
how she thanked Anne
think how

I wish Mom being so strong
didn't just remind me
of when
she was doing so much worse.

So Much Worse

That day,
      my thirteenth birthday,
she had been sober
for more than a month—
long for her—
      but then she got dumped by her alcoholic boyfriend
      he told her she was "no fun" anymore
and she said she had to have some champagne
to spite him and
to celebrate the birth of her little girl.
The fact that I was now actually
a teenager.
It made her cry.
How grown up I was.
How she missed her little girl. Her shadow.
She said if I went with her
she would buy me whatever I wanted
from the mall.
I told her I didn't care.
All I wanted for my birthday was for her to *not drink*.
But she refused, so I went with her,
knowing this way she'd be safer.

We went to this new Mexican place,
      big sombreros spinning on the walls,
      oversized margarita glasses.

I told her she said champagne.
At least when she had champagne,
I thought, she usually got a headache
and passed out.
The bubbles, she would say, groaning.
But liquor?
Anything could happen.
She said though it didn't matter really
as long as there was a kick to it.
As if I wasn't smart enough
                to keep track
                to know the differences
                between all kinds of drunk.

To distract her from a sip,
I asked her if she would buy me
new jeans like Cassidy's.

She said:
Whatever you want, baby.

But one margarita spilled into
another.
And I didn't even know where she got all that money.
Some other new guy?
The waiter kept asking me why I wasn't in school.
Noon on a Thursday.
I kept saying I was sick that morning.
Then I got better.
I kept coloring

a Mexican mouse
even though I was too old.
And she kept ordering.
Six.
Seven.
I told her *party over.*
Time for my jeans.
But then she said we had to have cake.
To celebrate.
And when she said it,
in between sips,
she told me the story I loved:
      the day she met my dad.
      How he made her feel like a balloon
      had been blown up in her chest.
      How she thought she'd float away with him.

Except she never finished the story.

Nancy the mall security woman came.
Asked me again why I wasn't in school.
Again.
It wasn't the first time she had seen us here.
Mom told her to mind her business.
Shouted a racial slur.
Like Nan would have done.
I apologized for her.
She grabbed my hand, led me out of the restaurant.
As we ran, past those jeans in the window of American Eagle,
Nancy chased us.

Mom slipped once,
but I lifted her up.

We kept going.
We were fast.

We ran out into the parking lot.

A woman was pulling out of her spot.
She pulled out too quickly
or we were moving too quickly.

She almost ran me over.

And Mom started screaming at the lady.
The lady got out of her car, slamming her door.
I tried grabbing Mom, calming her down.
But the woman said she was a "drunk idiot."
       And then Mom spat in her face.
       And the woman grabbed her.
       And Mom punched her.
       And then Nancy was there.
       And Mom shoved Nancy.
       And then one of the cops, when they showed up.
       And I watched the whole thing

And there was nothing I could do to stop it.
The whole world
       pulsed—and then bled—
       orange.

Finally

As we pull up
to Anne & Carl's
sturdy stone house,
I let Mom's sober, full smile fill me.
Try to make my own "amends."
   Maybe
that day in that parking lot
was what we needed.
   Maybe
if she hadn't lost me,
she wouldn't be in rehab.
Her smile would still hang crooked.

Just because I'm not with her,
doesn't mean I'm not
   helping her.

Balancing Equations

At school,
everyone's talking
about Audrey's holiday party.
What they will wear,
what they will bring her.
Audrey and I are paired
together in math.
I can tell she's surprised
I know so many answers.

> I used to buy my own math
> flash cards, workbooks
> from the dollar store.
> It was something I could do
> to keep the school's hawk eyes off me.
> If I kept up, Mom couldn't get into that much trouble.

At least I thought.

We balance equations.
At the end of class,
Audrey says Anne & Carl
usually come to the party.
She doesn't ask,
just says
she will see me there.

Drifts

In Worship & Ministry,
we all make a list
of sample favors
kids could do for each other
for our holiday event.
Think how Mom and I kept it simple:
doing dishes, making beds.
> But how one time I asked her to pour out her liquor,
> as a favor.
> She screamed at me that that was a waste
> of good money.
Push the memory aside.

We split into two groups,
5th & 6th graders and 7th & 8th graders.
Mariah says: *Bake cookies.*
I think about what it would be like
to grow up with a parent who bakes.
Jake suggests: *Help someone study for a test.*
I notice he doesn't look to Lauren
for approval like he usually does.
He just stares at his hands.
Lauren says: *Get their lunch for them?*
I write it down on our list.

It is snowing a bit outside
      and all of us
            seem to be watching the snow drift
more than working on our list.
Gordy, Oscar, and the 5th-grade girls
are all shouting ideas to one another.
But the four of us are quieter.

After the meeting,
Lauren asks again if I'm OK,
if I'm mad.
And I tell her no,
though thinking of Amy's unicorns
and stuffed animals,
I think I am angry.
At her? At myself?
But I can't tell her how I feel.
It will make everything worse.
She says:
"Well, if you are.
Don't be.
It'll all be over this weekend.
I promise."

"So, sooner than a month?"
That feels better.
To give Amy her room back. Sooner.

I nod my head,
            smiling now,
maybe it will all work out:
        Lauren will stop stealing,
        Mom will be sober now forever,
        and Anne & Carl can be my friends.

A place to visit.

Maybe I can visit Mariah, too,
eat cookies.

I ask Lauren,
does she want to hang after school.
Play in the snow?
She cracks a smile,
            we link arms
we float   drift together   down the noisy hall.

LAUREN

Not OK at All

The snow started up again on Friday morning—not enough for a snow day but enough to distract everybody in advisory, until Ms. Meadows held up a plastic bowl filled with folded-up pieces of paper.

"Instead of the Secret Gifters exchange we usually do, the Worship and Ministry group has organized a different kind of swap this year," she announced. "Lauren, would you like to tell us more?"

I glanced over at Sierra, who was running a finger back and forth along the edge of her desk.

"Actually, I think Sierra should. Unless she doesn't want to."

Sierra stiffened when I first said her name, but then she relaxed her shoulders and sat up straighter in her chair. "No, I'll do it."

"Yeah, Daisy!" Max Sherman called from the other end of the room.

Ms. Meadows shot Max a "quiet down" look before nodding at Sierra, and Sierra took in a big breath before she started to explain the Favor Swap. She balled her hands into extra tight fists, but she didn't talk too quietly for anybody to hear, like she used to when she was new.

Every time I talk in advisory, Audrey refuses to look anywhere near me, but she was looking at Sierra while Sierra told everybody all the details, and the expression on her face wasn't even mean. It's not like I want Audrey to scowl at Sierra, but still. Now it's only me Audrey has a problem with? When did that happen?

"And if you don't really know the person whose name you get that well, you can find some favor ideas on the bulletin board outside Mr. Ellis's room," Sierra finished. "Oh, and you should keep it a secret which person you pick until after you've done the favor, because it'll be a lot more fun that way."

Ms. Meadows beamed at Sierra and thanked her, and when Sierra looked back down at her desk and started running her fingertip along the edge again, I could tell she was holding in a smile.

"I'll just add that the only possible reason you might need to put back the name you pick and try again is if you pick your own name. And no reactions when you see who you get, please!" Ms. Meadows said as she carried the bowl to Max.

Of course, that didn't stop Max from groaning when he saw the name on his piece of paper. The bowl made its way around the room, and when it was Sierra's turn, right before mine, she had to put back the first paper she took, which meant her name was still in there.

Sierra. Sierra. Please let me get Sierra, I thought as I reached in.

Then I wouldn't have to use one of those simple,

works-for-anyone favors we'd brainstormed at Worship and Ministry. I could come up with something just for her. Something special that could maybe make her feel like at least she's made a friend who's *almost* as good as family, even if she can't be with her real family for the holidays.

I pulled out a folded-up piece that looked about the same size as the one Sierra had just dropped back in, and then I had to swallow back a gasp when I read the name.

Audrey.

I'm sure the only favor Audrey wants from me is to skip her family's holiday party, which obviously won't work, since that party is the key to me selling a bracelet for $300 and making it to $1,000.

But then I realized, I didn't need any of the works-for-anyone favors for Audrey, either, because even though Audrey and I aren't speaking, I probably know her better than anybody else. So I know the perfect favor to do. And the best part is, doing it will get me right across the hall from her mom's jewelry collection.

"Who do you have?" I whispered to Sierra on the way out of advisory.

Sierra's mouth dropped open. "Lauren! The whole point is not to tell!"

I pretended to pout, even though I knew she was right.

She swatted my arm with her notebook and said, "Outlook not good for our Favor Swap if everybody tells. Then there won't be any surprises!"

I laughed and answered her in Magic 8 Ball speak. "It is decidedly so. I know. I won't ask you again."

We grabbed our stuff for Spanish, but then as we walked

down the hallway toward the classroom, Jake was there just a few feet away, drinking from the water fountain.

One time right before we went to Mariah's, he was getting a drink at this same water fountain when Sierra and I passed the eighth-grade advisory rooms, and I reached up and flipped the hood of his sweatshirt over his head. He laughed the big kind of laugh that showed me all his molars and flicked water at me.

Today, he was wearing the same sweatshirt, but I couldn't imagine pulling his hood up over his head again. Because now, anytime I'm near him, I remember what he said when we were walking home from Mariah's. And then, it's like a hole opens up in my stomach and tries to swallow my lungs.

The thing is, I want Jake to think I'm a good person, but I know he wouldn't understand what I'm doing. And once I think of that, I can't help thinking of how Sierra doesn't want me to do it anymore, either, and how I don't want to make Sierra unhappy, but I also know I can't stop. Unless I get to $1,000, at least.

Jake finished drinking from the water fountain and picked up his head. He smiled when he saw me, but it was a confused, just-trying-to-be-polite smile, not the giant grin I used to get.

I tried to make my mouth smile back, but I knew I'd have to say something when I walked by him, and I couldn't talk with all that lung sucking, mind spinning going on. It's just too confusing, remembering the way he touched my arm and the nice things he said and being almost sure he likes me, or did before I freaked out, anyway, and knowing for absolute sure that I like him . . . but also knowing that I hated how I felt after he said what he did. Because it made me doubt myself too completely, and I don't have room for more doubt in my head right now.

So I stopped in front of the girls' bathroom. "Tell Señora I'll be there in a minute," I told Sierra.

Then I pushed open the door and stumbled in.

That night, the last Aveda shampoo and the last Anthropologie hair clip sold.

That meant after I got them back from Sierra, there'd be nothing left hidden in Amy's room. It also meant we'd made it to $733. We'd be over $1,000 as soon as I had the bracelet.

I was planning to mail the shampoo and hair clip on Saturday, but then right when I was about to leave, Mom and Dad came down the stairs.

"We're heading off to do some errands in Chestnut Hill!" Dad announced.

"But don't worry," Mom added. "We'll be back in plenty of time for the Lees' party!"

Dad put his arm around Mom and then winked at me and acted all exaggeratedly secretive as they got their stuff to go, which meant they were probably doing Christmas shopping for me and Ry. But shopping in Chestnut Hill meant they'd be right by the post office.

I texted Sierra as soon as they left to tell her I'd mail the stuff on Monday instead, but Sierra showed up at the front door twenty minutes later, holding Seeger's leash in one hand and a plastic bag with the shampoo and hair clip in the other.

"I already took them out of Amy's room," she told me. "I

really don't want to put them back in there, Lauren. Can you figure something else out? Please?"

Her lips quivered, and I got the terrible feeling she might cry if I said no.

"I guess *you* could mail them instead of me," I offered, but that didn't make her lips stop quivering.

She sighed. "I can't take Seeger all that way when it's this cold. And Anne will want to know where I'm going."

So I grabbed my coat and the bubble wrap I keep at the back of my closet. "OK. We'll walk Seeger around the block first, take him home, and then we'll go together. You can tell Anne we're going to get hot chocolate or something, and then you can stand guard at the post office so my parents don't catch me."

She didn't seem so thrilled about that plan, either, but she couldn't think of anything else, so she agreed.

I've been going to the post office every week for ages now, but Sierra's eyes went wide when we walked up, the same way her eyes had gone wide when she saw the inside of Audrey's house and my house, too.

"This is a *post office*?" she asked.

And for the first time, I paid attention to the big shiny gold doors and the elegant storefront. I guess that's how used to fancy stuff I've gotten. Even though I want to, sometimes I don't notice when something's ten times fancier than it needs to be.

I held one heavy door open and followed Sierra inside, where the line snaked around and around.

"At least it looks like a regular post office inside, anyway," she said, and I was relieved for some reason. As if I were somehow responsible for the post office's fanciness.

"Here, just stand here at the front and tell me if you see my parents so I can duck, OK?" I told her.

It's not like they were going to peer in the windows looking for me, so we just needed to make sure they didn't happen to walk by when I was in the part of the line that went closest to the doors and windows.

"How long do you think this will take?" she asked. "Anne's going to wonder if we're gone too long."

I couldn't really tell, though, because it's never this crowded when I come on weekdays.

I pushed my way through the line to the mailing supplies area so I could choose the right size Priority Mail boxes and fill out the labels. Most of the other customers were only there to mail holiday presents, but I knew exactly where to go for the supplies I needed, so I got on line fast. Still, it was taking forever.

As the line inched forward, I leaned to the side so I could catch Sierra's eye and stick my tongue out to make her laugh. But then a tall, dark-haired woman opened one of the post office doors right when I stuck my tongue out. She stepped directly in between me and Sierra, so it looked like I was sticking my tongue out at her.

My cheeks burned, and I wanted to hide behind the girl in front of me, who was wearing a hat with a puffy pom-pom on top. But the woman looked kind of familiar. Maybe she was one of the women Mom had started doing Pilates with this year? Or somebody's mom from school?

That hole deep in my stomach opened up a tiny bit. She *was* somebody's mom. She was *Jake's* mom.

I had accidentally stuck my tongue out at Jake's mom! I asked the pom-pom hat girl to save my spot in line for a second and rushed over.

"I'm so sorry, Ms. . . ." but I trailed off, because I still didn't know if her name was Paterson or Willis or both. "That's my friend behind you, and I was sticking my tongue out at her. Like, as a joke. I'm really sorry."

Jake's mom just looked at me for a second, studying my face as if she had no idea who I was, and then she threw her head back and laughed. A big, molar-showing laugh, just like Jake's.

"Lauren, right?" she said. "I won't take it personally. When Jake's sister was three or four, she used to stick her tongue out at everybody. I think I'm immune to the effect now."

I laughed, too, even though she'd sort of just compared me to a three-year-old.

"OK, well, say hi to Jake for me," I said, just to have a way to end the conversation and get back to my spot in line.

But she nodded a little too eagerly. "I'll do that, Lauren. And I know he's planning to make that Black Forest cake for us over the holidays. Maybe you can come over and help."

"Maybe so," I said, even though the lung-sucking stomach hole gaped farther open at the thought.

But maybe I *could* hang out with Jake again without freaking out by the time he made the Black Forest cake. If tonight went the way I hoped, I *could* be the best person Jake knows again, without having to give up on my plan.

If Jake still wanted me to be, anyway.

• • •

Audrey's mom grew up with conservative Korean parents who refused to make a big thing about Christmas. According to Mrs. Lee, they never got a tree, they barely bought any presents, and they wrinkled up their noses at the idea of eggnog or Christmas cookies or caroling. So now, Audrey's parents still make Korean food and keep up their Korean traditions for most of the year, but in December, Mrs. Lee makes up for all the Christmases she didn't get to celebrate when she was a kid.

The Lees have a massive tree in their front room that looks professionally decorated, and Mrs. Lee and Audrey string lights and garlands everywhere. For their holiday party, they hire caterers, and Mrs. Lee spends a whole week making little wreath and candy-cane cookies decorated so perfectly that it's impossible to believe she didn't buy them at a bakery. When we were little, she even helped Audrey transform the dollhouse in her room by decorating every tiny room with miniature wreaths and trees.

Audrey and I used to start planning our holiday party outfits weeks before the party, but this year I didn't think about what I'd wear until Sierra and I got back from the post office and she asked me what "festive fabulous" means, since that's what it said on the invitation.

"I don't think I have anything," Sierra said, so I let her borrow the sparkly green shirt I wore when I was with Audrey's family for New Year's last year. I ended up wearing the same dark red dress I'd worn to last year's holiday party, with black tights since now it's a little short.

Mom had on a brand-new emerald-green silk blouse with flow-y pants and a chunky green and gold necklace. I don't remember what she wore last year, but I do remember I heard her complain on the way over about how she hadn't had time to get her highlights touched up and Mrs. Lee and all the other women would look perfect. This year, she did, too.

When we got to the party, Mrs. Lee opened the door. I examined her jewelry and let out a long, relieved breath. No swirly silver bracelet on either wrist. I hadn't seen her wear it for a long time, but on the drive over, I'd convinced myself that tonight she might.

But I couldn't feel relieved for long, because Mrs. Lee pulled me in for a hug and held on tight. She smelled the same way she always smelled—like vanilla mixed with some kind of flower.

"We've missed you around here, Lauren," she told me. "I was so disappointed when Audrey said you can't join us for the ski trip this year."

"I just don't want to be gone when Ry's home," I said, but my throat got a little tight. I *always* go with the Lees on their trip to the Poconos over New Year's. It's not like I thought Audrey was going to invite me, but the fact that she hadn't asked and lied to her mom about it still made me sad.

Mrs. Lee nodded. "I can understand that," she said. "I was hoping he'd be back in time to play the piano for us again today."

Then somebody else arrived and rang the doorbell. "Make sure you get some chicken fingers," she told me before she greeted the new guests. "We got that honey-mustard dipping sauce again."

"Thanks, Mrs. Lee," I squeaked out past the tightness in my throat.

Dad had already wandered away to find one of the waiters

passing trays of pigs in blankets and cheesy pastries, and Mom accepted a bubbly red "house cocktail" when another waiter offered it to her.

"I think I see my friends," I told Mom, even though the only people I saw were Audrey and Emma, who wore matching sparkly earrings, and Max Sherman with a couple of other boys. Carl had some kind of meeting at the co-op where he works, so Sierra wouldn't be there for half an hour at least, and Audrey hadn't invited the whole grade. There was no chance somebody like Mariah would show up to talk to me.

Audrey whispered something to Emma when she saw me, and then the two of them scurried upstairs. I couldn't get anywhere near her mom's room with Audrey and Emma across the hall, so I took a seat on the couch next to Max.

His hair was combed and a little bit slick looking, and he had on a sweater over a collared shirt. He was bouncing one leg up and down hard enough that the soda he was holding sloshed around in the cup and came close to spilling.

"So what happens at these things, Loco?" he asked. "I see the Lees haven't started setting up menorahs or putting out dreidels for their Jewish guests."

"Yeah, not so much," I said. "Not the most PC holiday party ever."

Max shrugged. "I'll get over it if you tell me we still get to fish for presents."

I laughed, because I'd forgotten about the present fishing. This was the first year boys had been invited since we were in second grade, and back when we were little, Audrey's mom decorated a sheet to look like water with fish swimming around in it. She and my mom held it up, and Dr. Lee brought out his fishing pole. All the kids got to take turns "fishing," and Dr. Lee had to kneel behind the screen and slide little presents onto each kid's hook.

"Sorry, Max. The present fishing stopped a while ago." I gestured around the room. "It's pretty much just this. There's a big buffet in the dining room once it's dinnertime. And usually there are Christmas carols. Dr. Lee will probably play the piano."

Dr. Lee always used to play before Ryan took over last year. He's not as good as Ryan, but he's not bad.

I glanced at the Lees' piano across the room, where Ryan had sat on their cushiony black leather bench with his back perfectly straight and his face serious, rocking toward the keys and back as his fingers flew and notes rang out.

Everybody at the party had clustered around, applauding after each song and calling out requests. People requested holiday songs at first: "We Wish You a Merry Christmas" and "Jingle Bells" and "Winter Wonderland." And then harder stuff, once they realized he could play pretty much anything he'd heard.

"Do you know any Rachmaninoff concertos?" one of Dr. Lee's friends asked, his voice a little too loud and jolly.

I could tell he was trying to stump Ryan, and I clutched Audrey's hand. But it turned out I didn't have to worry about Ry.

He just nodded. "My aunts have a 'Best of Rachmaninoff' CD," he said, and then he was off.

"Go, Ryan!" Audrey cheered, and Ry's mouth curled into a smile, even though he didn't look away from those black and white keys.

Now Max took a sip of his soda and then set it down on

the coffee table. "Ah, well. Do you think Dr. Lee knows any Hanukkah songs? I'd better start to warm up my vocal cords just in case."

He started singing some shrill "la-la-las."

I shook off the memory of Ry at the Lees' piano and Audrey being nice.

"Sounds like you need a lot more warming up," I told Max, and the other guys laughed.

At the edge of the room, somebody made a clinking sound, silverware tapping a glass.

"Oh, and Mrs. Lee always starts the party off by telling the story of Audrey's first Christmas," I said. "That's our cue to gather around and listen."

I figured Max would groan the way he had when he picked a name out for the Favor Swap, but instead he nodded.

"I remember the story. They all fell asleep because they were so tired from taking care of Audrey and the food all burned, right? And three fire trucks came because their fire alarm went off?"

"That's pretty much it, yeah."

"Welcome, welcome!" Mrs. Lee called.

"It's a funny story," Max told the other guys. "C'mon."

They headed over to Mrs. Lee, and Audrey and Emma came back down from Audrey's bedroom to stand next to Audrey's dad.

I took a deep breath. This was the best chance I was going to get.

Mrs. Lee was right next to the front stairs, but I could walk around to the kitchen and go up the back way. I went nice and slowly, so I wouldn't look suspicious. In the kitchen, the caterers were so busy stirring sauces and piling appetizers onto trays that nobody even looked at me as I passed through. I was going to tell them somebody was in the downstairs bathroom and I really needed to go, but I didn't even have to say anything.

I went up one step, two steps, three steps, and nobody noticed me. When I got to the top of the stairs, my whole body was thrumming with adrenaline. I was really going to pull this off!

I went to Audrey's room, and, sure enough, neatly folded piles of laundry sat at the foot of her bed. Audrey's housekeeper does all the laundry, but Audrey's supposed to put hers away, and she never does. Sometimes her housekeeper caves and does it for her, and sometimes Audrey's mom notices and makes her do it. But most of the time, Audrey just ends up moving the clean piles down to the floor and picking out what she wants to wear from there.

We shared clothes for long enough that I know where everything goes, so it only took me a minute to put away her T-shirts, jeans, and pajamas. I left the underwear on the bed because it seemed too weird to touch that, and I paused for just a second when I put away the pajamas, because that's how Mom had ended up finding all the stuff I'd hidden.

Audrey would probably hate this favor. But it was my alibi for being upstairs in case somebody noticed I was gone, and I couldn't waste any more time taking everything out and putting it all back on the bed. I had to get to Audrey's parents' room. So I left an *I hope you like your favor* note on Audrey's bed where the clothes had been and tiptoed across the hallway.

I hadn't been in Dr. and Mrs. Lee's room since Audrey and I stopped playing dress-up with Mrs. Lee's fancy things, but everything looked the same as I remembered. Same soft beige comforter and big floral pillows on the bed. Same tall dresser next to the windows and same paintings on the wall. I walked over to the smaller dresser, with tiny drawers for necklaces and bracelets and earrings, and I stopped when I noticed the framed pictures lined up on the top.

One of Dr. and Mrs. Lee at their wedding, and Audrey's school picture from first grade—I recognized both of those. But there were three new photos I hadn't seen. One of Audrey and her parents at the beach, maybe two years ago. A more recent one of just Audrey, standing in front of the big tree in their front yard. And then one from last New Year's. My last Poconos ski trip with the Lees. Audrey and I had our arms around each other, and I was wearing a pointy party hat. Dr. Lee was next to Audrey, and Mrs. Lee was next to me, and they both held out champagne glasses as if they were toasting the person taking the picture.

I picked up the photo. We looked so happy, Audrey and me. That night, we'd met two kids from New York City and convinced them we were sisters but I was adopted. We told them our names were Simona and Jade. And we went back for seconds on ice cream sundaes at the resort's buffet, and we got so hyper from the sugar high that we couldn't fall asleep for ages, even after midnight. It was our best New Year's Eve ever, and it was less than a year ago. If someone had told me that night that Audrey and I would stop being friends this fall, there's no way I would have believed it.

But Audrey and I don't have anything in common any-more. And she tried to leave Sierra out when Sierra obviously needed friends. And she barely wanted to talk about Ryan after he left even though she was *Ry's* friend, too.

And, yeah, her mom gave me a nice hug and still smells the same and probably ordered honey-mustard dipping sauce just because she knows I like it. But her mom also has more jewelry than she could ever wear, even if she wore something different every day. She probably wouldn't notice the bracelet was gone, just like Audrey didn't notice *her* bracelet was gone. She'd probably be happy that I could help someone by selling it. She organizes lots of charity events for people who don't have enough.

But she keeps a photo with me in it on her jewelry dresser. And she really seemed sad that I'm not going away with them this New Year's.

Maybe $733 could be enough? Or maybe I could get Worship and Ministry to do another fund-raiser in the spring and find a way to have the money go to Jenna and other OTs like her?

But my fingers itched to open the drawers, and the idea of leaving this room without getting that bracelet—just giving up a chance for $300—made my hands shake and something ugly rise in my gut.

Downstairs, Dr. Lee started playing "Joy to the World" on the piano, and the doorbell rang. I'd been up here way too long now. I needed to make up my mind and get out of there.

I'll open one drawer, and if the bracelet's there, that means

I'm supposed to take it, I decided. *If it's not, I won't check any other drawers. I'll go back downstairs and try to forget it.*

I slid open the second drawer from the top on the right side on the dresser, and there, right on top, was the swirly silver bracelet with gold coiled around the edges and two blue stones facing each other.

So I took it. I had to.

I felt that same old easy-to-breathe adrenaline rush as I left Audrey's parents' room. My last year's dress might be a little short on me now, but the good thing is, it has pockets. I held my hand over the left pocket, pressing the bracelet in place against my hip as I jogged toward the back stairs.

Once I got the money for it and sent it off on Monday, I'd get to see the look on Jenna's face when I delivered more than $1,000. And then, if I ever started worrying that Jake might find out what I'd done and stop thinking I'm a good person, I could just remember that look.

I was practically skipping when I got to the stairway, until I saw Audrey, starting to come up.

Her chin stuck out so far, it must have strained her neck muscles. "What are you doing up here, Lauren?"

I closed my fingers around the bracelet in my pocket.

"And don't lie and say you came up here to use the bathroom, 'cause I was standing right near the one downstairs, and nobody's been in it since Mom's big speech," she added.

I gripped the bracelet tighter through the fabric.

"Check your bed, Audrey," I told her, offering up a silent thank-you to the universe for giving me that little piece of paper with Audrey's name on it when I reached into Ms. Meadows's bowl. "I was doing you a favor."

I didn't show Sierra the bracelet until the very end of the night, when I had to give it to her so she could hide it at home. I wrapped it in one of Mrs. Lee's gold-rimmed paper napkins, even, so Sierra wouldn't have to know what it was if she didn't want to.

"This is it," I told her. "The last thing I'll ever ask you to hide. You can bring it to school on Monday, and I'll take it to the post office right after."

I thought she'd be happy, but she let out a long, shaky sigh as she held out her hand for it. She didn't say anything—she just nodded once and then followed Anne and Carl out to their car.

I was happy, though, because I took a picture of the bracelet when I went into the downstairs bathroom at the Lees', and the guy who wanted it for his girlfriend paid me right away. And Sierra would be OK as soon as I took the bracelet back from her. I could even think of an extra special favor to do for her, to help her have an OK Christmas. Who cared that I didn't pick her name?

But then the next morning, Mom knocked on my door.

"You didn't see any kids going upstairs at the Lees' house, did you?" she asked. "Any of those boys who were running wild by the end of the party?"

I'd been about to start my English reading, and I dropped my book onto the floor.

"I . . . I don't think so. Why?"

Mom shrugged. "I got an e-mail from Audrey's mom. Looks like something went missing during the party, and she's trying to figure out if anybody knows anything. She thinks it might have been one of the caterers, but she doesn't want to make any accusations if she's wrong."

I could barely hear the end of what Mom said over the echoing pounding of my heart.

Mrs. Lee knew the bracelet was gone already? What if she blamed the caterers and somebody got in trouble—fired, even—for something *I* did?

But Mom hadn't said anything about the bracelet, specifically. Maybe something else was missing, and one of the caterers *did* take it.

"Lauren?" Mom said. "You look pale. Are you OK?"

But suddenly, I wasn't OK at all.

SIERRA

Dulled

When Lauren handed me the bracelet
my body washed blue
like when I would pour Mom's bottles out
but then she would buy, find another.

There was always another.

When I went to hide it,
the box
under Amy's bed,
the silver bracelet
looked blue, too,
all its shine rusted

cold.

Fate

Anne asks me
if I know anything about a missing bracelet.
She got an e-mail saying
Audrey's mom's in a panic.

I tell her no.

As she leaves, though,
I know what I need to do.

The stealing, the hiding
              is bad
but it's worse
to have it there,
with Amy.

I wait until Anne's footsteps fade
press my door
back open.

Chance

Standing in the hall,
I hear Anne put on the teakettle,
Carl cough as he turns the newspaper.
I take my chance.

Open Amy's door quietly,
crawl back under the bed.
Hand on the box, then around the bracelet.
Pulling it toward me.
When I hear Seeger barking.
Sniffing at my feet.

I'm sliding back out
hand still on the bracelet
when I hear Anne say:

"Sierra!
What are you doing?"

Disappointment

I don't need an 8 Ball now to tell me
what to do.
I'm going to leave here.
Lauren has to stay.
There's only one person
here
I need
to protect.

I tell Anne it is my fault.
I took it.

I tell her I'm sorry
for hiding it with Amy,
it was the only place
I thought
no one would look.
As I say it,
my eyes focus on one of
Amy's unicorns—
        it looks like it's in a parade
        prancing
        flags flying from its horn.
Carl comes in then,
puts his hand on Anne's back.
She rubs her temples.

She doesn't lecture me,
or yell
Carl shakes his head,
says softly they need to discuss this,
        together.
They will come back
        to talk to me.
They leave me there
with the proud unicorn.
I think about going to the closet.
Getting all the money, too.
Showing it all to Anne.
But I see Lauren watching then
from the window.
I've already disappointed them.
How can I disappoint her, too?

Leave the room, the unicorn
and his proud prancing.

Focus

Back in my room,
I ignore a GIF Cassidy sent me
of our old Disney Channel crush
smashing his face into a pie.
I have more important news.
I text Lauren.
Tell her I did her a favor,
after all I am her Secret Gifter:
You probably saw.
Got caught. Took the blame.

It feels familiar covering for her,
like all the times I'd call in for Mom—
      pretending she was sick
      and couldn't work.
      Pretending I was sick
      and couldn't go to school.

Lauren texts back:
Oh no.
You didn't have to do that.
I can tell them.

But then her whole plan would be ruined.
And she would be in so much more trouble.
And me?
I'm gone
as soon as Mom can get me.

I write back:
NO. I'm leaving soon.
My mom's coming to get me.
Sorry about the $300.

She texts back:
Did you get caught with the money too?

I tell her no.

Shame spirals through me.
What would Anne think of me
if she knew all that money was there, too?

Shove it out of my mind,
hold my kaleidoscope, turn the dial
focus on the future:

      Mom will get me back
      and we'll move to
      the new apartment complex,
      Brighton Acres.
      Spend next summer
      in their gated pool,

laugh at how they tried to split us

a   part

        but we wouldn't budge.

Text Lauren back:
Don't worry.

Lauren asks again: Are you sure? This is OK?
And then in 8 Ball speak,
my mind on Mom, the pool,
the kaleidoscope's spinning green swirls
I type:

Outlook good.

Decidedly So

Anne says
we need to walk to Audrey's.
    I need to give back
    the bracelet,
    apologize to Mrs. Lee.

It is decided.

My stomach flips.
I don't want to do it.
But better me than Lauren, right?

As we walk,
Lauren is outside.
Says hi to Anne,
then pulls me aside.
Asks if I'm sure about this.
The wind blows her hair all around,
she doesn't even have a coat on.
I tell her, yes, I am. I am sure.

"I get to leave—
but you have to stay."

She bites her lip.
Turns around.
I put my head down.
Close my eyes, see Mom and me again in the pool.
On rafts, laughing, holding hands.
Our rippling reflections.
I move
            steps, inches
                    forward.

The wind picks up.
Snow drifts.
Anne follows.

Already There

They're already all there.
At the front of the house,
they knew we were coming.

No one yet has asked me *why*.
Maybe they all assume
it is because I'm not rich
like the rest of them?

Like it would be so hard
to be around all their things
and not want them for my own?

But what I want isn't about things.

Anne puts a hand on my shoulder.
I'm surprised she touches me,
she must be so angry at me.
At what I have done
to Amy's room.
She doesn't even know
what I'm still
doing.

Anne
places the bracelet then
in my glove.
I pass it to Mrs. Lee
say I'm sorry for taking it.
Mrs. Lee nods
thanks me for returning it.
Audrey squints her eyes at me,
like I am a bug she's studying
under a microscope.

Her cheeks pink in the cold.
I whisper a sorry to her, too.
But from her face
it looks like she may never
accept.

Crowding

Lauren apologizes again on the bus.
I tell her to stop, I'm OK, happy, even.
I'll probably be gone within the month.

I cross my fingers when I say it.

Right off the bus,
the first people we see,
Audrey, Emma, Max
crowding in their circle.
Whispering.

Lauren looks at me again
before she leaves for class.
She's out of earshot
when
Emma loudly says the word

thief.

Appearances

At lunch,
Lauren sits with me,
Mariah stops by,
her hair now bright yellow with orange tips,
says she heard what happened,
that that sure doesn't seem like me.
Lauren coughs.

As she stands above us,
I think of what Audrey said
during that Meeting in October,
what Anne must think of me now,
how I thought Lauren seemed perfect
when I first met her.
I shrug, say:
"People
sometimes aren't
who you think
they are."

Not sure if I feel guilty or proud
when Mariah frowns.

Switch

Max usually talks to me
        more than I ever talk to him
          I pretend to not like it
          but maybe I do

but today

    all he says
    while we are crammed together
    as classes switch
    is
"Move."

Under my breath
so he doesn't quite hear it
I say:

"Soon."

Stops, Starts

I'm a little late coming home from school,
so much traffic on the Avenue.
Lauren got picked up early for a dentist appointment.
So, I'm alone.
Think of texting Cassidy
how excited I was to come home soon.
But then picture her telling me I'm lucky.
Instead—
Send her an emoticon of two girls dancing.
Listen to Dad's old playlist,
count:

> bare branches,
> piles of dirty snow,
> each time the bus stops, starts.

> My breaths.

Home,
Anne says I missed
a caseworker call.
Must be an update on her new job, home.
Maybe I will be home before Christmas?

Now I wait by the phone,
pray to Mom
for luck.

Count the seconds
before the phone rings again.

But the way Maude says,
Hello, dear,
I can tell—
like winter's brown grass—
and all those red lights on the way home—
all my green's run out.

Stuck

"Your mom's relapsed, Sierra."
She asks if I know what that means.
Like I'm a small child.
"So sorry.
It may take longer than we hoped.
I guess right after discharge she met someone—"
Like I haven't been through this before.
"I don't know when she'll be ready."
      I don't need her to be ready. I just need her to be her.
"You need to settle in there."
      Can I settle in with Mom drinking again?
"Carl says you've been in some trouble.
I strongly advise you not to get into any more."
I don't know how to get out
without losing Lauren,
the only thing I have
here.

Complexes

Maude speaks with Anne.
Anne tells me she is so sorry,
asks do I want to talk about it.

How can she still feel bad for me
after what I've done to her?

I ask if there's any way
I can stay
home from school
tomorrow.

"A mental health day?"
she asks.
I nod.

I'm grateful Anne recognizes
how much I need it.

Later that night,
I hear Lauren come to the door.
I haven't answered her texts.
I know she feels ignored.
Or is worried about the money.
She texted that she has a plan

to get something again
for the last $300.

How could she still want to do this?
I bury my head under the covers.
I hear Anne say
that I need some time alone.

Falling asleep,
I walk the halls of our old
apartment complexes.
Pass vending machine after vending machine,
try to remember which doors were ours.

Protection

The next day,
Anne lets me watch Netflix on her computer.
Makes me grilled cheeses,
and doesn't make me answer any questions.

It makes me want to hug her.

Carl comes home early from work.
He says he wants to take me somewhere.
Handing me a bike helmet he says,
"You'll need this."

Breaking

Anne gently hands me an old bike.
It's pink and a little small for me.
I put on the helmet, even though
Mom would've never made me.

I don't argue.

Carl rides ahead of me.
We cross a bridge.
The cars speed past us.
I tighten my grip.

We
wind down
roads through an apartment complex.
　　　The wind picks up.
　　　The sun disappears.
　　　The trees grow denser.
　　　The road steeper.
Going fast now,
　　　　　　down.

I feel the fear like the moment before I know Mom's lost
　　control,
and there's nothing I can do to save her.

My breath quickens
all I can think is
I need to save her.
I slam on the brakes.
Crash.

Fall.

Bandaging

Carl turns back.
My knee banged and scraped.
My hand bleeding.
I curl in.
Fight back tears.

He pulls bandages, Neosporin from his fanny pack.

"What do you say we walk awhile?"

I nod. We park our bikes.

Limp down the rest of the road.

And there's a river.

Alongside it
the trees whisper.
Inside it
geese honk.

Stones shine in the sun.

I think how much Mom would like it here. How she loves
    moving water.
Carl tells me this is called Forbidden Drive,
where there are no cars allowed.
My hand throbs.
My knee stings.
I don't ask to sit but Carl
guides me to a bench.

In the quiet,
my mind sings
"You Are My Sunshine."
My mom used to sing it to me
when I was little
and got hurt.

You'll never know, dear, how much I—

But Carl interrupts—
"We're happy you're with us, Sierra."

The bare branches quiver
and I stay quiet, still
not sure what to say back.

My Fault

Anne picks me up from the woods
in her car.
Throws my bike into the back.
Says she's sorry I got hurt.

Would she be sorry if she knew it was my own fault?

I only got hurt
because I braked   suddenly.

Mom would probably yell at me if she was here.

Tell me I am always worrying about   nothing.

Our whole lives one big
Brake.
Crash.
Fall.

Stunned

In the afternoon,
the doorbell rings.

I look to Anne.
Her eyes widen.
She smacks her forehead.
She forgot, she says.
Audrey's here for another lesson.
        So much for a mental health day.

Anne's hands in a chicken she's preparing for dinner,
I get the door.

Before Audrey goes to the craft table,
she says:

"I know you're lying for her.
Lauren hasn't been the same since—
she's not the same person anymore."
                        Then—
"Sorry for Max and Emma the other day,
I told them it wasn't you."

I don't know what to say,
so I step back, stunned,
hand and knee still hurting,
I head back up the stairway.

So Much More

I almost throw up
on my way.
So scared for Lauren,
for me.

I feel like I did on that bike.
The world moving so fast, it wouldn't stop.
It's all my fault.
Just like that day with Mom,
I should've made her stay home
and not take me to the mall.
I should've never gone into Amy's room
to move the bracelet.

We would've never gotten caught otherwise.

I go to text Lauren,
to warn her,
but my hand slips,
knocking my kaleidoscope to the floor.

And the tears don't stop,
as I sort through
the shards of mirrors,
        all the pebbles,
                bits of glass,
                all that I have left
                of my mother.

Finding

Anne finds me there,
crying,
sits down next to me.

She tells me
none of Mom's choices
are my responsibility.
My mom has a disease.
It is so much bigger than me.

She tells me
she's going to take me to AlaTeen.
I need to meet kids
with stories like my own.

She tells me
Audrey has a theory
she just shared with her.
That I wasn't working alone.

She picks my chin up then,
makes me look into her eyes.

Says:
"Sometimes, the best thing we can do for anyone
is to let them fall.
This is the best—maybe the only—way to help them."

I thought Mom's fall
        going to jail
would help her
        it almost did

but maybe she still
hasn't fallen hard enough.

Maybe it isn't enough just to lose me to make her better?
Maybe she has to want it
for herself.

I think of falling off the bike.
How it hurt, but I did stop the bike myself.
By falling, I stopped the momentum.
The out-of-control feeling.
I saved myself
even though it hurt.
Look down at those splinters of glass, the beads.
Think how many pieces go into
making those swirling colors.
So much goes into making them spin.

Think about Lauren's pieces.
How she's so strong in her convictions
but how I've been worried about her, too.
I leave the mess there.

Walk into Amy's room. Anne follows me,
to the place with all Lauren's money.

"It's Lauren's.

She has a problem.
She needs help,"

I say,
trying not to look in Lauren's window,
I keep my eyes on that parading unicorn.

LAUREN

Restitution

It was Sierra's idea to take the blame for the bracelet, and she'd promised she wasn't mad. But she wouldn't talk to me when I went over Monday night, and she didn't answer any of my texts when she was absent on Tuesday. And then on Wednesday, she didn't sit with me on the bus home from school. She got on so late, I didn't think she was going to make it, and then she took a seat right up front, next to a sixth grader.

As soon as the bus stopped at the end of our street, she sprinted straight home without even looking back at me, and then I saw Dad's car. Parked in front of our house hours and hours before he should have been home.

He and Mom were in the study with the door closed and their voices fast and quiet—piling on top of each other's but too soft for me to understand.

Ryan. Something must be wrong with Ryan. What if they decided he wasn't coming home for winter break after all?

I went to my room, and I wasn't surprised when Dad called up the stairs for me a little while later. They were going to break it to me, I figured. That we weren't having Christmas as a family after all.

I wasn't even surprised when he yelled up a second time, thirty seconds later, saying, "Right now, please, Lauren!"

But I *was* surprised when I followed his voice into the living room. He and Mom were sitting together on the smaller couch, just like when Mom found that stuff in my pajama drawer. But this time, the bigger couch wasn't empty.

Anne and Sierra were there, side by side, with Anne's arm linked through Sierra's and Sierra's head bent so far down that I couldn't see her face at all.

"Sit down, Lauren," Dad said in his lawyer voice. Absolutely definite.

The big couch is long enough for way more than three people, and Anne and Sierra were sitting so close together that it left extra space, technically. But the way they huddled together made it feel like there wasn't any room for me at all.

"Now," Dad added.

So I sat, as far away from everybody else as I could. Right up against the arm of the sofa.

"Anne came to talk to me today, Lauren," Mom said. Her eyes were red, and she held a balled-up, makeup-stained tissue in the hand that wasn't gripping Dad's.

At the other end of the couch from me, Anne cleared her throat. "I told your mom about Mrs. Lee's bracelet, Lauren, and a very large sum of money that was hidden in Amy's closet, and several other stolen items."

The TV was off, but the cable box was still on, and green numbers glowed on the display. I stared at those numbers while I tried to understand what Anne was saying. None of it made any sense, because Sierra had covered for me. I hadn't even asked her to, but she had. And nobody knew about anything other than the bracelet. Sierra had specifically told me Anne hadn't found the money.

"I had to tell," Sierra squeaked then. "Everything. I'm so sorry."

And it's not like my skull suddenly weighed more than usual, but it took extra effort to pull my eyes off those numbers on the cable box and turn my head toward Sierra. I could only see a wall of mostly straight blond hair, slightly wavy at the edges. She needed a haircut to even out her ends. That's the thought that went through my head.

"I know you want to fix things that are messed up," Sierra said. "I know you want to make things fair. But it's like you can't stop now. It's scaring me."

I forgot about split ends and haircuts, and that hole that sometimes sat at the bottom of my stomach opened up so wide, my lungs couldn't function at all. *Scaring* her? What happened to partners in justice? We were supposed to be a team!

And, what, it just didn't matter that I'd spent all fall making sure she wasn't stuck by herself at lunch or on the bus or in advisory? Trying to get her to smile a real smile instead of that fake one? Didn't that mean she should talk to *me*, not Anne, if something was wrong? Didn't that mean she owed me *anything*?

She looked over at me for just a second, and her brown eyes were so sad that for that one moment, I wanted to stay her friend more than I wanted to be mad at her. But then she turned away. Away from me, back toward Anne.

"Sierra?" Anne prompted, and Sierra took the white envelope full of money out of her sweatshirt pocket and set it down on the coffee table.

The stack was thick now, not thin like the pile of bills

Mom had found soon after I got started. It was obvious that there was a lot of money there. Enough money to make some kind of difference.

"That's everything," Sierra said. "Seven hundred and thirty-three dollars."

Anne started to stand. "Sierra and I should go. We'll leave you to talk as a family."

On the other couch, Mom sniffled, and Dad leaned his head back and stared at the ceiling.

A family. What a joke. What kind of family are we without Ryan?

Sierra bolted out of the living room, but Anne stopped and gripped both my hands. I thought she'd be mad at me for making Sierra take the blame for the bracelet, even though I hadn't. Or for being a bad influence or a bad friend. I flinched as she leaned in close to whisper.

But she just said, "Talk to them, Lauren. Tell them how you're feeling. Let them help." Then she gave my hands a squeeze and followed Sierra out the front door.

Mom, Dad, and I were all quiet for a minute after the door thudded closed. Mom took another tissue out of the box on the coffee table and held it to her face, dabbing the edges of her eyes so her eye makeup wouldn't smudge any more than it had already.

"I should have realized something was wrong when I found those things in your drawer," she said, looking straight ahead, out the window into the backyard.

Brown, leafless trees, browning grass peeking out from under the graying leftover snow. That's all there was to see out there.

"Or before then, even," Mom went on. "I just . . . you *stole*, Lauren. That's a *crime*."

Dad stood up so fast that the toe of one of his shiny work shoes slammed into the leg of the coffee table. His heavy footsteps echoed as he stormed into the study. He came back with a legal pad and a black pen, which he shoved at me.

"You're going to write down every single thing you took and sold and where every single thing came from," he said. "And I will walk this list next door and ask Sierra if anything is missing, so you'd better not leave anything off."

"But . . . but people already have the stuff I sold," I pointed out. "It's too late to—"

"It is certainly *not* too late for you to make some serious restitution!" he shouted.

I wasn't sure what *restitution* meant. Usually I ask when he uses a legal term I don't know. Usually he loves to explain. Tells me it's a sign of intellectual promise, being curious about things I don't know.

But right then, I couldn't ask him anything because of the terrible way he was looking at me. With *disgust*. Like I was worse than those criminals he prosecutes because I was his responsibility. Tears leaked out the corners of my eyes.

"Right now, Lauren," he said, a little softer but just as definite. "Let's go."

Mom pushed the tissue box toward me, but I wiped my eyes on the sleeves of my sweater and started the list.

1) Lucky jeans (mine, from Mom)
2) Brian Dawkins jersey (mine, from Dad)
3) Silver cuff bracelet (Audrey's)
4) Cuff links (Walkers' yard sale)

How was it even possible, how right it had felt to take each one of those items on the list and how wrong it felt to write down each of those words with Dad looking over my shoulder and Mom crying on the little couch?

"I know that's not all, Lauren," Dad said.

I left off Mom's ring and the Fitbit, since he already knew about those. But I kept on writing the terrible words, showing him the terrible things I've done. The terrible person I am.

5) Shampoos (Aveda at the mall)
6) Ring and hair clips (Anthropologie)

Not a person with a great sense of social responsibility, like Mr. Ellis had said at the first Worship and Ministry meeting. Not a helpful sister, like Jenna had called me. Definitely not the best person Jake knows.

7) Cashmere sweater (Aunt Jill's that she gave me at Thanksgiving)
8) Dress from Aunt Jill's 40th birthday party (mine, too small)
9) Boys' shoes (Ryan's, too small now and never worn because they pinched)
10) Perfume (Mariah's)
11) Swirly silver bracelet (Mrs. Lee's)

When I was finally done, Dad sent me up to my room. Anne had said to talk to Mom and Dad, but they didn't give me a chance.

Mom came up later, to bring me a bowl of pasta and a

glass of seltzer water. She kissed the top of my head and said, "We'll get through this," but then, right away, she turned to go.

The next day was the second-to-last day before winter break, but just before my alarm went off, Dad came in to announce I wasn't going to school and he wasn't going to work. He made me write a note to every single person or store I'd taken something from and checked each one.

He took the money I'd made from selling the jeans, the jersey, Aunt Jill's sweater, my old dress, and Ryan's old shoes. Then he made me stuff each apology envelope with the money I'd made selling whatever I was apologizing for taking. Except for the note for Audrey's mom, since I'd had to refund the money for the bracelet and she had it back. And I had to add some of my babysitting money to the Aveda and Anthropologie envelopes, since I didn't sell that stuff for as much as it cost.

As soon as the mall opened, Dad drove me there and dragged me into the Aveda store.

"My daughter has something to say," he told the tall, pale-skinned woman behind the counter.

Her lips were painted dark red, and I focused all my attention on how precisely she'd filled them in with color. Those exact, curving lines where the darkness of her lips met the paleness of her skin, like in a coloring book but without any black borders to stay inside.

"I took some shampoo," I said. "From your store. I'm very sorry."

But it was hard to *feel* sorry standing in this store, where

one giant wall was lined with hundreds and hundreds of bottles of shampoo and conditioner and hairspray and gel—more
than anybody would ever buy. I held out the envelope labeled
AVEDA, but she didn't reach out to take it from me.

She pressed her dark red lips together and rubbed them
around, but the color didn't smear.

"There's no shampoo inside that envelope, is there? Looks
a little flat." She said it like she was making fun of me. Like she
thought this whole thing was a joke.

"Um, no," I told her. "I sold it."

I studied the rows and rows of skin-care products on
display behind the lady. Moisturizers. Toners. Eye cream. So
many different kinds of lotion that people think they need.

Better to focus on all those lotions than on Dad sighing
next to me as his phone buzzed with work e-mails, or on this
Aveda salesperson who thought I was a joke.

"This is money to pay for it, though. And, um, there's a
note, too. To say sorry."

"Look, kids steal stuff from time to time." She looked me
up and down before she continued. "For the rush of taking
something, mostly. Sometimes we catch them, and if we don't,
that's that, you know?"

"It wasn't for the rush!" I protested. There *was* that easy-
to-breathe adrenaline jolt after I took something, yeah, but
that wasn't really why I did it.

Dad tore the envelope out of my hand. "Take it," he ordered
the woman.

Then he pulled me out of the store and led me straight
past the food court, where we always, always stop for

smoothies—mango, strawberry, banana for me and berry blast for him—and back to the car. I'd barely eaten breakfast, so my stomach rumbled loudly, but Dad ignored it.

As he pulled out of the parking lot, he turned on sports radio. Two guys were complaining about the moves the Eagles' coach had made in the last game and freaking out about how they're not going to win on Sunday if they can't run the ball better, and how the defense has been underachieving.

I thought of the Dawkins jersey I'd sold and the look on Dad's face when he saw it on my list. The rumbling in my stomach switched over to something sharper.

"Nega-delphia, right?" I said, pointing toward the radio speakers.

That's what Dad usually says when we're listening to sports radio and the people get extra negative, saying the Eagles' season is over after one little thing goes wrong. *Philadelphia fans are the most informed fans in sports but also the least optimistic*, he used to tell me.

But this time, he didn't say anything. He just switched the station to music.

"Restitution" went a little bit better at Anthropologie. Dad didn't give any money to the homeless guy sitting a block away from the store, but I slipped the guy a quarter from my pocket. And the older lady at the front counter smiled sympathetically when I explained why we were there. She thanked me for my "courage," even though being dragged by Dad didn't feel very courageous, and then she said she tells the managers it isn't a good idea to put out sale bins on the counter.

"Too much temptation," she said.

But that wasn't right, either. It wasn't *temptation* that made me take things.

Dad drove me all the way back home even though we were right near his office. Then he left me with Mom and took the train back downtown to work.

"The Walkers' house, then the Freedman-Taylors' house, and then the Lees'," I heard him instruct Mom before he left. "And I want her to apologize face-to-face, not just leave the envelopes."

I ate leftover pasta for lunch and tried to hurry Mom up to go to Emma's and Mariah's and Audrey's houses before they'd be home from school, even though technically I was supposed to apologize face-to-face to Audrey and not just her mom. But Aunt Jill called, and then somebody from Ry's school called about the plan for picking him up for winter break, and by the time we finally left, it was way too close to the end of the school day.

Neither of us said anything for most of the walk to Emma's house, but when we got to her street, Mom spoke up. "Anne said you wanted to give the money to Jenna."

I looked down at the uneven slabs of the stone sidewalk and remembered the first time Sierra had pointed out all the stone in Mt. Airy. *Stone Central*, she'd called it.

She'd be getting out of Stone Central pretty soon now. I wondered if she'd be back at school after winter break or if she'd just go off with her mom for Christmas and never come back. I wondered if she'd even say goodbye.

"I just thought she could make a difference with it. For kids like that girl Hailey."

I thought I'd have to remind Mom who Hailey was, but she nodded. "You've always had so much compassion, Lauren. It makes me sad that you stole. It scares me, really."

There it was again. Me being so terrible that I *scared* somebody.

"But I know you," Mom finished as we walked up to Emma's house. "You're going to find a way to do something great with all that compassion." She paused before she knocked on the door. "Something *legal*."

Emma's little brother answered the door and ran to get her mom. I peeked inside, and I didn't see Emma anywhere, at least.

"Kate! Lauren! What a surprise," Mrs. Walker said. "Would you like to come in?"

"You're sweet to offer when we just show up unannounced," Mom said, "but this will only take a minute."

So Mom wanted to get out of there just as fast as I did.

"Lauren?" she prompted, and I held out the envelope with Mrs. Walker's name printed on the front.

"I'm really sorry," I began. At least I had the spiel down by now.

Mrs. Walker was more confused than anything else when I explained what I'd done and gave her the money. She said she hadn't noticed the cuff links were missing—she'd just assumed her husband had sold them. But apparently she was planning to donate what they made from the yard sale to a homelessness charity, anyway, and she said she'd add the money to what they already had.

"Looks like you got a lot more for the cuff links than we would have asked," she joked when she looked inside the envelope. "I should hire you next time we have things to get rid of."

Mom let out a strangled laugh and said we had to be going, and I was glad Dad wasn't there. He wouldn't have found that funny at all. Mariah's house is only a couple of blocks away from Emma's, so we walked up Mariah's front path a few minutes later. I was kind of hoping her dad Jonathan would answer, but Mr. Freedman was the one who came to the door. I was pretty sure I could hear Mariah and her sister inside, but at least they stayed wherever they were.

Mr. Freedman was way angrier than Mrs. Walker. "I welcomed you into our home, taught you to create a beautiful meal, and fed you delicious food, and you opened up our bathroom cabinets to look through our things and then took something from us?" he said once I apologized.

There was nothing I could say to that except "yes" and "I'm sorry" again. But Mr. Freedman was wearing one of his aprons and busy getting dinner started, so I didn't have to stand there feeling awful for very long before he thanked my mom for bringing me and said he needed to check on his soup now, and goodbye.

As angry as he'd been, I couldn't feel too relieved as we walked back down the Freedman-Taylors' front steps and started off toward Audrey's.

"This last stop will probably be the hardest, huh?" Mom said.

Mom, Ry, and I used to walk this route together back when I was too young to be allowed to walk by myself. Ryan liked to come because Mom usually got him a treat from Starbucks or the bakery on the Ave., and he would notice every car we passed on the whole walk over. Sometimes he'd count how many brand-new cars we saw and how many we saw that were ten years old or older. Then he'd list all the safety features the new ones had but the old ones didn't, and Mom would joke that that was why she and Dad leased cars: She'd live in fear of all the safety features we didn't have if we didn't upgrade to a new model every few years.

"The dealership is grateful for your expertise, Ry," she'd tell him, and he'd nod, even though she was mostly being silly.

Last year, Mom and Dad had started letting me walk to Audrey's by myself, but I always noticed all the cars anyway, even without Ryan there to point them out. I didn't know enough to tell how old every car was, but sometimes I'd count red cars or black ones or silver. When Aunt Jill and Melody stayed with me while Mom and Dad took Ryan to North Carolina over Labor Day weekend, I'd walked to Audrey's, sure that if anybody could make me feel better, it was her. That day, I'd cried the whole way and counted blurry blue cars as I passed them.

But then once I got to her house, she just asked if Ryan liked the going-away gift she and her parents had gotten him—a soft fleece blanket with his initials sewed into the fabric—and then she didn't listen when I said I didn't think he should have gone.

And then that was it. She didn't ask why I didn't want him to go or how I was feeling or what it had been like, saying goodbye.

She lined up all her new fall clothes on her bed and asked

me to help her pick her first-week-of-school outfits. And when I didn't want to do it, she said I could borrow her new polka-dot shirt for the first day, since Mom hadn't had time to take me back-to-school shopping yet. She *seriously* thought that would make everything OK.

And now, I hadn't walked this way since the day we were supposed to make Halloween costumes but then Audrey freaked out and Sierra and I left. That day, red and orange leaves had crunched under my feet as I walked down these sidewalks. Now, a thin crust of old snow covered the grass that peeked through the stone slabs.

I'd been so sure I was right at Halloween, when I wouldn't let Sierra switch costumes just so Audrey could get her way, and when I told Audrey she didn't deserve me or Sierra after she, Emma, and Max dressed up as the Fates. I'd been so sure I was right to sell her bracelet when she didn't even notice she'd lost it. But now?

Dad's supposed to love me no matter what, and he was disgusted by me. I was so twisted up inside that even when I tried to do something good, I disgusted one person who's supposed to care about me and scared two others. I couldn't imagine what Audrey was going to think once she knew what I'd done. She hated me already.

We made it to the Lees' tall stone house, which is set back from the road and up on a little slope. Their front yard isn't a big hill, really, but it was big enough for Audrey and me to go sledding in the winter when we were little and to lie on our sides and roll down in the summer, crashing into each other at the bottom, all covered with sweet-smelling grass.

I didn't pause at the bottom of the hill. I marched right

up, because if I stopped, I'd never be able to make myself start going again.

"Their cars aren't here," Mom said, panting a little as she followed me.

I rang the doorbell anyway. Maybe just Audrey was home. Maybe I deserved to face Audrey by herself, without Mrs. Lee, who would probably feel bad for me and maybe forgive me.

But nobody came to the door. Mom stepped up next to me and put her hand on my back, so gently I could barely feel it through my coat.

"I think we can leave the envelopes, if you want," she said. "You talked to all of the other people. And we tried."

That wasn't what Dad had told her, but I nodded and slid Mrs. Lee's apology note through the mail slot in their front door.

I held on to Audrey's envelope, though. I deserved to have to give her that in person.

On Friday morning, the hallways were packed with girls giving out holiday gifts to their closest friends, even though the rule is no distributing gifts or invitations at school unless you have one for everybody, and boys rushing around doing last-minute favors for the Favor Swap. Max Sherman grabbed Grace Millinowski's books out of her hands to carry them into advisory.

"Favor complete!" he announced as he pushed his way through the crowd toward Ms. Meadows's room. He pumped a fist, and two of the books slid out of his hands and hit the floor. I felt a little bad for Grace, since she knew Max had groaned when he picked her name out of the bowl.

Nobody was going to do a favor for me today. Sierra had done mine already, even though it barely counted now, since she'd changed her mind and told Anne what I'd done. And nobody had any holiday gifts for me, either.

Audrey had to know by now that I'd taken her mom's bracelet—maybe she'd even figured out I'd taken hers, too. That probably meant everybody else knew, too. And maybe Mariah knew about the perfume and Emma knew about the cuff links.

At lunch, Sierra took the last empty seat at Mariah's table and leaned down so far over her food that all I could see was the side part in her hair. I just stood there with my tray, trying not to look like I was searching the cafeteria for a place to sit.

"Coming through, Loco! Watch it!" Max Sherman said, bumping me in the back with the side of his tray. I gave up and took my food to Mr. Ellis's room, where he let me eat by myself while he graded papers.

He asked me about my plans for break and thanked me for all my leadership in Worship and Ministry, but luckily he didn't say anything about my strong sense of social responsibility or how my passion could really make a difference. I think I would have lost it if he had.

After English class in the afternoon, I saw Audrey walk into the bathroom by herself, so I pulled her envelope out of my bag and followed her in. I was waiting for her next to the sinks when she came out of the stall.

She froze between the stall and the sinks when she saw me, like maybe she'd rather take off without washing her hands than have to deal with me. She crossed her arms around herself extra tightly, the way she always used to do during the scary part of a movie. As if she needed a hug, so she was giving herself one.

"I took your bracelet," I told her. "The thick silver one you left at Starbucks when we met there back in October. I sold it, because I was trying to raise money for people who need it. I'm really sorry."

She took a step forward, finally, and held her hands under the soap dispenser.

"I know we're not . . . you know. Best friends anymore, or any kind of friends or whatever," I added. "But I shouldn't have taken your bracelet."

She rubbed her soapy hands together under the faucet, so hard that little bubbles flew up and stuck to the mirror.

"And my mom's bracelet, too?" she said.

So she did know.

"My mom *cried* when she read your note, you know. And she almost cried when I told her you weren't coming to the Poconos this year. That's how much she cared about you, Lauren. And then you went and *stole* from her."

Tears gathered in the back of my throat, gagging me.

"And you know why we aren't friends anymore? Because you *changed* this fall. Suddenly nothing I did or said was good enough for you anymore, and you liked Sierra better than you liked me. We didn't just stop being friends, OK? You did that."

She leaned around me to grab a paper towel to dry her hands, and I wanted to tell her that nothing *anybody* did or said had felt good enough after Ryan left. I wanted to tell her how upset it had made me every time she'd tried to talk me

320

out of worrying about Piedmont. Every time I'd brought up Ry and she'd changed the subject to something that didn't matter.

She was probably right, though. Nothing she had done was as bad as what I'd done. I set the envelope down on the edge of the sink she was standing next to.

"I really am sorry," I told her, and then I walked out into the loud, crowded hall.

I made it through my last class before break and kept my head down as I walked toward Ms. Meadows's room to pick up my backpack and jacket. Too many people cheering about vacation, saying, "Let's definitely hang out this weekend!" and, "Text me while you're away!" and, "See ya next year!"

When I got to the space outside the classroom, I looked up, and Jake's hopeful, confused brown eyes looked back at me. He was standing right there, waiting.

"My mom said she saw you at the post office," he said. "She said she told you I'm making the Black Forest cake and maybe you could come help. I'll probably do it on Sunday, if you're free."

I pushed up the sleeves of my sweater, which suddenly felt scratchy. "My brother's actually coming home from boarding school that day. I may be pretty busy."

I couldn't look up at him when I said it. I didn't want to see his eyes turn disappointed.

"Listen, I'm sorry if I freaked you out with what I said after Mariah's," he said. "I just . . . I try to be honest with people about what I think. But I didn't mean to embarrass you. I promise I won't say stuff like that anymore. I want us to be friends still."

Embarrass me? That was so far from the truth that I

almost laughed. "Do you want to know what kind of person I really am? I stole a bunch of stuff from my parents and my friends and even a couple of stores, and then I sold it to make money for therapy for kids with autism. I actually believed I was doing something *good*—that's how messed up I am."

I reached around him to grab my stuff.

"You don't want to be friends with me. Trust me," I said, and then I walked right out the back door, sat down on the bus, and stared straight out the window as all the happy kids piled on. Nobody took the empty seat next to me.

SIERRA

Just for Today

Watching Lauren struggle
        not knowing where to sit
                when she helped me fit in
        not reaching out to her
        not helping her
was one of the hardest
things I've ever done.
I bit my lip
        crossed my fingers
        counted the tiles in the cafeteria
anything to stop myself
from rescuing her.

Anne says I need to stop
rescuing.

She says that is *my*
addiction.
I never thought about it like that
that I was just as addicted to

pouring Mom's bottles out
as she was to drinking them.

That it was a system.
Now,   broken.

That
just for today
I can make a different
choice.

Free Will

When I go into the AlaTeen meeting
in the basement of the church
there's a big sign on the door:

The Three Cs:
>   *Can't change it*
>   *Can't cure it*
>   *Didn't cause it.*

I read it over twice,
then open the door.

The first person I see
surprises me.

Emma.

I almost turn around
walk out of the room.
She's eating cookies and drinking lemonade
with a few other kids
I don't recognize.
She waves to me.
I sit down next to her,
tentatively.

We begin.

The leader,
a Latina woman named Sue,
says welcome to me, specifically.
She asks if I want to tell
my story.
I look around
all their faces
staring at me.
I tell her not right now.
She nods her head,
other kids talk.
One boy says he had to drive his dad home
from a holiday party
even though he doesn't have a license.
Another says he's so happy
his grandmother's been sober a year now.
And then Emma says,
her dad's working the steps
and for the ninth one,
where they have to make amends,
he admitted he was very drunk
the night of the school play,
so he didn't get to see her play the lead.
He had lied and said he was sick.
Emma in her big fancy stone house.
Emma who whispers with Audrey at school.
Emma has a parent who drinks and lies, too.

I think of all my mom's lies.

A design starts to form in my head.
Colors all in a mix.
My heart speeds up.

All those years
my mom taught me that the color I saw
made the day that was meant for me.
But:
Maybe she was wrong.

Maybe I create my
destiny.
Maybe I'm not just one color, one mood,

I am so many things.
But there's also a lot I can't do.

     I can't stop Mom from drinking.
     I couldn't stop Lauren from stealing.

But I can do something.

I do it before I lose my nerve.
I raise my hand.
Sue says I don't have to, I'm not in school, just talk.

"My name's Sierra,
and my mom is an alcoholic.
My dad—he's an addict, too."
She looks at me as if I might say more.
But I don't.
But maybe
someday
I will.

Gratitude

After the meeting,
        Emma says maybe we can hang out
        sometime at school.
But she also reminds me
        not to tell anyone she saw me there,
        and she won't tell *anyone* about me.
Then she surprises me
        and says Lauren came to her house
        to give her mom some money
        for something she stole.
And Audrey said
        Lauren was the one who stole
        her mom's bracelet,
        she delivered an apology note.

I nod at her,
I know she's apologizing
for calling me a thief.
        But I am thinking of Lauren.
She must have had to go
everywhere, return
all the money.

She must have been so embarrassed.
        I should've gone, too.
        I was responsible, too.

"I won't tell anyone about seeing you here,"
I say to Emma.
And she says, "Thanks, see you at school."
Then she says she's sending out invites
to her Bat Mitzvah soon,
that she hopes I'll come.

When Anne picks me up
and asks how it was
I say it was actually good.
I want to tell her more:
that Emma was there,
that so many of those kids
have stories like mine,
that even the cookies
were good.
Instead I squeeze her soft hand and say, "Thank you."

Something New

When we get home,
I tell Anne and Carl how Lauren
had to go everywhere
and apologize for everything.
I ask them if they think
we could still be friends?
Carl looks to the side
like the answer might be there
but Anne quickly says she does,
of course.
"But maybe not exactly like you were before,"
she says.
Carl nods.
Anne says, "Maybe you can make something new
together."
And I have an idea then.
I ask her if she will help me

And then she helps me
break pieces
glue them
make something
old into something
beautiful,
new.

Opening

On Sunday, Mom calls.
At first
I want to have Anne
talk to her
not sure what to say.
> But it is snowing hard
> which reminds me
> of one time Mom took
> Cassidy and me sledding
> on old trash can lids
> by the high school.
> And how fast we all went.
> Shrieking, speeding in the snow.
> And then how I got hurt.
> And Mom carried me back,
> sobbing,
> saying I was her precious girl.
I say, "Merry Christmas."
I can tell from her voice
she's been drinking.
She doesn't say sorry.
She just tells me
she's excited
she's bought me
new clothes,
a new iTouch,

something else I can't understand
for my new room.

I know somewhere in her heart
she believes all of that,
and somewhere in my heart,
I want to, too.

So I tell her that sounds great
and when I hang up,
tears falling,
Anne is there
with her arms open.

She whispers to me:
"I know I can't be your mom, Sierra,
but I can be your Anne."

And I nod,
knowing now
how much I need one of those.

Still & Moving

I ask Carl if
he will take me
back to the Wissahickon Creek.
Remembering what he said about being in nature
helping him.
He says he'd be delighted.
He has something else to show me there.
This time we don't go see the geese,
we walk down steps.

"Where are we going?"

I see the river ahead.
And he leads me.

      Down.

Out on a pathway over the water.
To sit on the dam.

One side the water is smooth.
On the other it ripples.

We don't do anything but sit
in the cold
and breathe.

I think how if Mom is the ocean,
Anne and Carl are more like this creek.

He doesn't pressure me to say anything.
To change or move.

Just says, "Sierra, whatever happens,
there's always a river to watch."

I nod,
breathing into its gray-blue.

Many Hearts

Later,
Cassidy texts, says Mom
has been hanging out
with some dude she met at Wawa
before she lost her job.

                              Again.
I think of Cassidy saying I was lucky to be here.
And, for the first time, I wonder if maybe I am.
Maybe she wasn't ignoring my problem
when she said that but, instead,
speaking her truth.
So, I tell her something honest, too:
I don't think I'll be home anytime soon.
She texts a sad face.
I think of her then—
              in the middle of her cluttered room
              her screaming sisters, her mom with some guy,
              the way they all fight over food.
And—
think of her saying she wanted to run away with me.

So I text:
Could she could sleep over
on New Year's?
I picture maybe Lauren
with us.

We have hats on and those honkers.
Candy and soda.
She texts me many hearts and a Christmas tree.

Says she can't wait.

Then she sends me a GIF
of some guy dancing
with a plant on his head.

And when I laugh this time,
I mean it.

Kaleidoscope

I wrap my present to Lauren.
I imagine her face
as she opens it.

Carl makes cocoa,
and the house smells like chocolate.
Anne is making gingerbread,
which used to be Amy's favorite.

I curl up on my bed.

Out the window, I look down at their garden.
Think about raking leaves when I first arrived.
How unfamiliar everything looked.
Now, I picture
      planting imperfect
      tomatoes,
      peppers,
      even kale
      learning how to garden following Carl's instruction.

Who knows, maybe one day, I'll be able to teach Mom.

I don't have Mom's kaleidoscope anymore.
So I close my eyes instead.

In my mind's eye
I see a kaleidoscope of faces:
          me
               Lauren
         Anne
   Carl
                  Mom
      Dad
       Cassidy
                Audrey
       Emma.

I watch us all spinning,
colliding,
disconnecting
and then connecting again.
     Like colors,
we all get our turns
          to fade away
 and to shine.

Anne calls my name.
"Time to pick up the tree," she says,
and I open my eyes.

Seeger jumps up
and follows me.
Together we bound back down
the old wooden
stairs.

LAUREN

Something Yellow

Dad and Ryan's flight was due in at five on the Sunday before Christmas. A little bit before six, we heard a car pull up outside.

Mom and I were in the kitchen, making a welcome-home dinner with all Ryan's favorite foods. I sprinted to the dining room to look out, but it wasn't Dad's shiny SUV outside the window. It was Carl's old sedan with a Christmas tree tied to the roof. He, Anne, and Sierra all got out, and together they untied the tree. Then Carl hoisted it over his shoulder and carried it around back while Anne and Sierra went up the front walk.

I ducked down so they wouldn't see me watching. Sierra said something that made Anne laugh, and Anne's laugh made Sierra smile. Just before they made it to their front steps, Anne reached over to put her arm around Sierra, and I realized: They look like family now, Anne and Sierra. It doesn't matter that Anne's skin is dark and Sierra's is pale. There was something about the way they walked up the front path together that made their connection absolutely obvious.

I walked out of the dining room and back to Mom then.

What was Anne going to do when Sierra went away? How much longer did they have together?

A few minutes later, Dad's car really did pull up. The rumble was closer this time, and when two doors echoed shut, one right after the other, Mom and I looked at each other and then ran toward the front door.

Dad came in first, carrying his small overnight bag in one hand and Ryan's bigger suitcase in the other. He kissed the top of Mom's forehead as he passed by to set down the bags at the edge of the living room, and I tried to tell myself the bags were just heavy, and he didn't kiss my head because I wasn't right in his path.

And then Ryan came inside. He was wearing his red winter coat, unzipped, and his favorite soft gray T-shirt and sweatpants. He's even taller than he was in October, so the shirt isn't as long on him as it used to be. His hair's longer than usual, too.

Ryan held one hand up, and Mom rushed over to take it.

"Oh, buddy. It's so good to have you home," she said, and then she completely lost it. Just started sobbing, right there in the hallway. "They're happy tears," she said. "I've just missed you so much."

Ryan leaned his head down so that it rested on top of hers for a second, and my eyes filled with tears, too.

Then Dad slid behind Mom and put his arm around her shoulders, and that terrible, terrible thought I couldn't ignore after Family Weekend, that maybe Mom and Dad thought life would be easier without Ryan? That's when I knew for absolute sure how wrong it was.

"My tears are happy, too," I told Ryan. And they were,

partly, but they weren't only happy. Because it was better, mostly, but also worse in a way, that Mom and Dad didn't *want* Ryan to go away, but they still sent him.

And after all these days and weeks I've spent wishing Ryan was home, now that he was, I had no idea what to say. I just froze there, a few feet away from him, until he smiled his familiar Ryan smile. He towers over me now, but he reached one hand down and tapped the top of my head twice before we pressed our palms together.

"Hi, La-La," he said.

"Hey, Ry Guy."

He looked good. A little thinner in the waist than when I saw him last, and he was standing up straighter than he used to. Like he was feeling a little more comfortable. A little more confident.

"Are you hungry?" I asked. "Or do you want to play the piano? Or should we go downstairs to see your fish?"

Ryan didn't say anything, so I kept on talking.

"The tank looks pretty awesome," I said, because the fish-tank guy had just come, so it was all algae-free. "You've probably missed your fish, right?"

Ryan took in a long, shaky breath. I'd thought for sure he'd want to do one of those things, but maybe I was wrong? Maybe I didn't get it anymore, what would make Ryan happiest?

You're always so tuned in to what Ryan needs, Jenna used to say, and it made me think of his piano in the living room—how happy it made him when we'd just had it tuned, and how he cringed and held his ears when it was time for the tuner to come back.

Had he been gone so long and changed so much that we were *out* of tune now? That I didn't know how to be his helpful sister anymore?

Ryan reached into the pocket of his jacket and pulled out something red. One of the laminated name tags Mom had told us about, after Thanksgiving. He held it up.

"Do you need a few minutes to yourself first?" Mom asked, and Ryan nodded.

"I need a few minutes by myself first," he said.

Dad still had one arm around Mom, but he reached out his other arm toward me. I took a step closer to him and let him pull me in.

It stung, Ryan not wanting to be with me right away. It stung a lot.

But this was what he had worked so hard on with Jenna—stepping away when he needed a break. Telling other people what he wanted instead of sticking out something that made him uncomfortable until it was too much and he melted down. This was what he hadn't been able do over the summer, when he visited me at camp, because he hadn't wanted me to be unhappy.

"Totally understandable, buddy," Dad said. "It's been a long day."

"You take as long as you need," Mom added.

Ryan flicked the fingers of his left hand, the one that wasn't holding the little red sign, and his eyes jumped up toward me and then back down. "La?"

Dad gently squeezed my arm, and I cleared my throat.

"We'll be right up here whenever you're ready," I said.

Ryan smiled then and headed down the basement stairs.

Dad kissed the top of my head, just like he'd done with Mom when he and Ryan came inside, and I leaned into him for a minute, letting my forehead rest against his chest in a way I hadn't done in ages. On the other side, Mom did the same thing. We're about the same height now, Mom and me, so my forehead came up at the same level hers did.

"He's home," I said, because for some reason I just needed to say the words out loud.

"He's home," Mom echoed. "He's really home."

And once Ryan came back upstairs, we all sat at the table together—Ryan back in his usual seat across from me—and ate our chicken fingers and mashed potatoes. The chicken fingers had gotten a little dried out from staying in the oven too long, and I'd put a little too much milk into the mashed potatoes, but none of us cared.

Ryan told us about how taking care of horses isn't all that different from taking care of fish in some ways, and how he doesn't mind broccoli and cauliflower when they're roasted, but he only likes to water the kale and beets—not to eat them.

And how he wrote a whole three pages about his compost project—the longest essay he'd ever written in his life—because he'd actually had something he wanted to say. And how much he likes being able to play songs based on how the notes look now.

"I thought you liked playing your way," I said. "Didn't you hate it when your old teacher tried to make you read music?"

Ryan's mouth curled into a smile as he pointed at my glass of seltzer water. "I thought *you* hated fizzy drinks."

I wrapped my fingers around the cold glass. "I . . . not anymore. That was when I was little."

"I don't hate learning to read music anymore, either," he said. "I like how this teacher explains things. And this way I don't have to wait to hear how someone else played a song before I can play it for myself."

I took a small sip of my seltzer, remembering how the bubbles used to tickle my nose, and I thought about all the ways I'd changed since I was a little kid who thought fizzy drinks were awful. Ryan had changed, too. Of course he had.

After dinner, before he headed upstairs to get ready for bed, Ryan held his hand out to me again, so I could press my palm against his.

"You seem really good, Ry," I said.

He nodded. "I'm happy. I told you."

And he had. When we were saying goodbye at Family Weekend. And he'd tried to show me in his video messages, too. I had been so focused on all the things I *thought* would make him happy that I hadn't listened.

And I guess this is the thing: It isn't just that Ry is working on telling us what he needs. I have to work on listening, too.

After Ryan and Mom had both gone up to bed, Dad called me down into the living room.

The Eagles game was on the TV, paused. "I recorded it this afternoon, and I managed to avoid spoilers," he said. "You didn't watch it yet, did you?"

I shook my head, and he patted the seat right next to him on the big sofa.

"Then want to join me?"

I'd already seen the final score, but I didn't say that. I just sat down next to him.

"Definitely," I said as he pressed play.

· · ·

The next day was Christmas Eve, and Mom was taking Ryan to visit Jenna at the OT center. She tried to get me to come along, but I couldn't imagine seeing Jenna again now—not after I'd spent so many weeks picturing myself giving her all that money. Then Mom tried to convince me to go next door to "make things right" with Sierra, but I knew Sierra wouldn't want to make up with me. That hole opened up in the pit of my stomach when I thought of all the little things she'd done and said to show me how much she hated that I was taking things and making her hide them, and how I hadn't listened to her, either.

"Let me stay here," I begged. "I won't go anywhere, I promise."

She didn't used to mind if I went for a walk when she was out, but I was still on punishment, technically, and I knew it was going to be a while before she trusted me again the way she had before.

She hesitated, but finally, after she called Dad at the office and found out he was leaving work in fifteen minutes, she gave in.

To be honest, when she and Ryan first left, there was a part of me that wanted to leave, too, even though I'd just promised her I wouldn't. I had at least forty-five minutes till Dad would be back, and I guess I sort of missed the thrill of doing something secret and against the rules. I could walk down to CVS and be back before Dad's car pulled up. I hadn't gotten gifts for anyone yet, and that way I could get everybody cards and candy canes for Christmas, at least.

I pictured all the Christmas stuff on the shelves in CVS. And then, without even meaning to, I pictured that aisle of overpriced makeup. So many different kinds of mascara— lengthening, strengthening, volumizing, whatever that means. So many different shades of lipstick. I imagined myself grabbing one mascara and one lipstick, sliding them into the pockets of my coat. It would be so easy. It would feel so good to walk out of the store with that secret.

But then my phone rang. Dad, calling to say he was stopping for milk and paper towels on the way home, and did I need anything else.

"Laur?" he asked when I didn't answer right away. "You there?"

I thought of that disgusted look on his face when he found out about the stealing, and then the way he grinned and gave me a high five each time the Eagles scored last night.

I shook off the idea of taking that CVS makeup and dug my fingernails into the palms of my hands, hard. What was wrong with me, even imagining that?

"I'm here," I told Dad, and I got an idea. "I could use a few ingredients, actually. Can you hang on a second while I find a recipe?"

That night, with a little bit of help from Dad, I made Mariah's dad's Black Forest cake. I couldn't wrap it up and put it under the tree for Mom, Dad, and Ryan to open, and I wasn't sure Ryan would like the way the whipped cream got mushed together with the cherries. But at least I hadn't bought stuff nobody would really want, and I had another idea for Ryan, anyway. Sheet music for Rachmaninoff's piano concertos—the ones Dr. Lee's friend had asked him to play. It should get here in time for New Year's.

When Dad and I finished icing the cake, it looked almost as good as the one Mariah's dad had helped with, except the layers didn't bake quite evenly, so the top was a little slanted to one side.

I took a picture of the slightly slanted cake, and before I could talk myself out if it, I texted it to Jake right before I went to bed. I felt pretty terrible about the way I'd avoided him and then run off without even giving him a chance to respond the last day before break.

Made the cake for Christmas dessert! Thanks for bringing me to your cooking lesson and sorry about everything after. Merry Christmas.

At least that way I'd apologized to him, too. I didn't expect a response, but the next morning, I woke up to one.

I didn't end up making it yet but yours looks great! A little nervous about messing it up. Maybe if you have any time you could come over and help?

And then a second one: Just to make sure I don't burn the kitchen down. And Merry Christmas!

My heart sped up as I read his messages. How could he still want anything to do with me after what I'd told him? He'd liked me because he thought I was a good person. Why didn't he hate me now?

But even though it scared me, I figured I owed it to him to give things a chance if he actually still wanted to. I could already hear Mom, Dad, and Ryan downstairs, but before I went down to join them, I texted a response.

Sounds like a safety hazard so I better come. Maybe next week?

The idea of him texting back and suggesting an actual day was a little more than I could handle, so I kept my phone on silent, set it facedown on my bed, and headed down to my family.

In the living room, in front of the Christmas tree, were two piles of neatly wrapped gifts: one for me and one for Ryan.

Ryan got some new rocks for his little fish tank at school, T-shirts and sweats in his favorite, extra-soft brand, and some books about Ancient Egypt and environmental science. He got a super-expensive pair of headphones, too, and I flinched as he opened them, because his old headphones weren't *that* old, and they still worked and all. The new ones did make him pretty happy, though.

When Ryan had opened all his gifts and started testing out the headphones, Mom and Dad told me to open my presents, too. "Start with that red one," Mom said.

So I pulled off the snowflake-printed paper to find a small old velvet jewelry box. Inside were delicate stud earrings with green stones and gold posts.

"They were your grandmother's," Mom explained. "Emeralds. Your birthstone and hers, too. I was waiting until you were old enough to appreciate them."

I rubbed a fingertip over the shiny round stones. Passed

down, not brand-new. Every time I wore them, I'd think about how Grandma once wore them, too, not about how much they cost.

"I love them," I said, and Mom smiled.

"Now the green one," Dad said.

Inside that box was a new Eagles jersey to replace the Brian Dawkins one I'd sold. It wasn't signed, and the back said our last name, Collins, instead of a player's name. And when I lifted it up, something fluttered out and landed in the box.

"Tickets?" I asked Dad.

"For the last game. Upper deck."

I got up to hug them both.

"Hey, wait," Dad said. "You have one more present to open."

My last gift was a small bag with two envelopes peeking out the top. I rummaged around for something else inside the bag, but all I felt was tissue paper. I picked up the thinner envelope first and read the return address.

"This is from Ryan's school?"

"Just open it," Mom said.

It was a thank-you note from the school's scholarship fund. "Did we make a donation?"

Dad nodded. "Mom and I donated the money you earned selling things that belonged to you and Ry, and we added a little extra. I know you already know that what you did wasn't right, but we're proud of you for wanting to help other people."

"The scholarship fund is for kids who would benefit from the program at Piedmont, but their families can't afford it,"

Mom added. "So they can have the same chance Ryan's getting."

And even though I still wish Ryan didn't have to go so far away, I'm starting to understand, a little. It was a big deal, the way he'd told us he needed a break the night he came home. And I like how he's excited about what he's learning, and how he talks about his friend Ellie and a guy named Curt, who loves music and plays the guitar.

"There's one more envelope," Dad said.

He and Mom were looking at each other and smiling as I pulled it out of the bag. I almost didn't want to open it, because I wanted to freeze this moment just how it was. Mom and Dad got it, what I'd been trying to do, even though I'd done it all wrong.

But finally, I opened the second envelope to find a plain card with a message in handwriting I didn't recognize. I scanned to the bottom to see who it was from.

"Jenna?" I said out loud.

I had to read through the note twice to be sure I understood it.

"This says I'm going to be volunteering with her on Saturdays?"

Dad nodded. "So you can help other kids with their social skills practice, just like you've always helped Ryan."

I looked over at Ryan, who was setting up at the piano with the music for the Beethoven sonata he was learning at school, and I remembered the time he'd learned that chorus song just for me so I could sing my solo. I had so many memories like that. Ryan listening to me practice my lower school graduation speech over and over and applauding each time. Ryan buying me a shark stuffed animal at the aquarium gift shop to make up for the fact that we hadn't gone to the zoo the way I'd wanted. Ryan lending me his favorite T-shirt the first year I went to sleepaway camp, so I could wear it to bed if I was homesick.

"Well, Ry's always helped me, too," I said. "We've helped each other."

"You really have," Mom agreed.

I cleared my throat. "Does Jenna . . . does she know what I did?"

Because now my old plan felt so stupid—so completely humiliating—and how could I face her if she did?

"Just that you want to do something good," Mom said. "Something that matters. And Dad and I think she'll be lucky to have you."

The thing is, it isn't really enough. I mean, I'm glad we gave money to the scholarship fund, and I'm glad I can work with Jenna. But I looked up how much Ryan's school costs. The money we donated will only pay for a tiny fraction of what it costs to send one person there, and what about all those other kids on the autism spectrum who might be going to schools where the teachers and therapists don't appreciate the things they do well, or they're getting homeschooled, or they're working with awesome people like Jenna but not as often as they want to. It's like those homeless people on the street—how there was no possible way to give money to all of them. And even if we could, it's not like one spare dollar would *really* change anything.

It's all still completely messed up, that I live in this big house with all this expensive stuff we don't really need and go to this school where most people's parents drive shiny new cars and buy them expensive stuff that they don't need, either, and then there are neighborhoods like the one in Northeast Philly where Mr. Ellis used to teach and even the one where Sierra came from. And even though I don't know what to do to make any of it less unfair, I do know this: I'm not going to forget about Hailey or zone out when I walk past somebody asking for money on the street. I *won't*. Because someday, maybe, I'll be able to do something more.

When I carried my presents upstairs, I flipped over my phone to see if I had another text from Jake. Instead, I had one from Sierra. My heart pounded as I read it.

I left something on your front steps for you. I hope you're having a really good Christmas with your family.

I shoved my feet into my furry boots and sprinted down the stairs.

"Lauren?" Dad called as I ran by the living room. "Is everything all right?"

"Uh-huh!" I shouted back.

I opened the front door and picked up the package, wrapped in simple brown paper with a shiny gold bow. There was a note taped to the front.

Dear Lauren,
    I'm so sorry you had to go by yourself to apologize and pay people back. It was my fault, too. It turns out I'm going to be staying longer with Anne

and Carl, and I hope that we can be friends again. I made you this gift because Anne says broken things make the best jewelry and my mom says yellow represents friendship. Maybe I can tell you more about my mom soon, if you still want to hear.

Love, Sierra

I ran my fingers over Sierra's words. My third letter of the day, and the most precious to me out of all of them.

I wanted to know why she was staying and how she was feeling about it and anything she wanted to tell me about her mom. And I wanted her to meet Ryan and read Jake's last texts and try a piece of my Black Forest cake. But most of all, I wanted us to be *us* again.

Or I wanted us to be the version of us that could walk Seeger together and stay up late asking the Magic 8 Ball questions and help each other come up with the best ideas for Worship and Ministry and make each other laugh in the hallway and wish for real potato chips instead of kale ones. If I could, I'd go back and erase the parts where I made Sierra keep hiding stuff when I could tell she didn't want to, and the part where she told Anne what I was doing and got me in trouble. But maybe it's better that I can't.

Maybe that's what makes two people family, even if they're not related—messing up and hurting each other but then figuring out how to change and heal and become OK again.

Mom peeked out the front door, holding a mug of steaming coffee. "What are you doing out here without a coat, honey?"

I held up the present to show her, but I covered the note, because that was just for me. "From Sierra," I said, and she smiled.

"Good. I knew you two would make things right."

I thought she'd tell me to open the gift inside, but she just took my winter coat out of the hall closet and handed it to me.

I slid my arms into the jacket and lowered myself down onto the top step, where I tore open the paper to find a bracelet. Not shiny silver like the ones I took from Audrey or her mom. This one had bits of yellow china flecked with tiny pink roses, rubbed smooth around the edges and strung together on wire like little shells.

Broken but transformed into something beautiful and new. Kind of like Sierra and me, maybe.

I put it on right away and tipped my wrist to the right and then the left, listening to the tiny pieces clink together. And just before I stepped back inside, Anne and Carl's front door swung open. Seeger scampered out first with Sierra behind him, holding the leash and wearing a new green winter coat.

I was still in pajamas under my jacket, but it didn't matter.

"Hey!" I called after Sierra. "Wait up!"

Acknowledgments

The first idea for this book came from my time working as a counselor intern at the Milton Hershey School, and a mobile therapist with Adams Hanover in Central Pennsylvania as well as the time I spent in Al-Anon meetings many years ago in South Carolina. I am grateful for all the people I spent time with in those places . . . and all the strength I witnessed in kids and adults alike.

Laurie, writing this book with you was one of the most joyous creative experiences of my life. All of it was so fun: the brainstorming, the writing back and forth, your thoughtfulness and attention to detail a perfect balance with my own bigger-picture thinking. You are undoubtedly one of the hardest-working people I have ever met, and Lauren is so lucky that she had you to give her a voice. I hope we stay friends and writing partners forever! A million yellow hearts to you.

Sara Crowe, thank you for your optimism and encouragement. Your honesty and advocacy mean so much to me.

Maggie Lehrman, I love that this story found its way to you. Your gentle direction combined with your upbeat enthusiasm has made this process smooth and energizing. I knew you were a great writer, whip-smart, and a caring friend, and now I also know that you are a fantastic editor. Thank you also to the entire Amulet/Abrams team.

Laura Sibson and Mary Winn Heider, thank you for

reading this story and helping it grow into a better book, never-ending gratitude for your support and kindness.

Megan Gantt, thank you for your enthusiasm and lending your counseling expertise to this book. Thank you to Kristie Gantt for answering questions concerning foster care and CYS.

Courtney, Roger, and Susan, you also might find glimpses of your story in Sierra, Anne, and Carl's journey. I am grateful for the time that we all got to spend living so closely together—as hard as some of it was. I know I am not present in the same way I was, but those years will always stay with me. I love you all.

To Mt. Airy, or as Sierra would say, "Stone Central," my favorite place I've ever lived. Thank you for being the welcoming place you are.

Jon, thank you for enjoying this story so much and caring about nature and the environment with such passion. We are all better for it. Thank you for always meeting me where I am and relishing in all the ways we are different. You are an incredibly giving and gifted partner.

Tate and Lily, you have been some of my best creative writing students. The excitement we all have for a good story is awesome. I could never invent any better kids than each of you; my love for both of you is unconditional and endless. Being a writer is great; being a mom is the best.

—CJ

Cordelia, the day you said "We should write a book together" was one of the luckiest days of my life. Thank you for believing I could tell Lauren's story and cheering me on every step of the way. I am in awe of your talent and creativity, and I'm so glad that Lauren has a friend like Sierra and that I have a friend like you.

Sara Crowe, thank you for your unwavering belief in my writing, your enthusiasm for this novel, and your dedication to finding it the perfect home. And Maggie Lehrman, from your very first email, it was clear that our book was in the very best hands. You understood our vision for the novel, and your calm, wise questions and insights helped us to realize it. And thank you to the Abrams/Amulet team for producing this beautiful book.

I am grateful to the entire Vermont College of Fine Arts community, especially Laura Sibson and Mary Winn Heider, wonderful writers and wonderful friends who gave us valuable feedback on this story; the whole Secret Gardeners class; and my four advisors: Alan Cumyn, Franny Billingsley, Mary Quattlebaum, and Shelley Tanaka.

Thank you to the readers, including Lyn Miller-Lachmann and Kristin Reynolds, who provided generous, thoughtful notes about autism, about Ryan, and about his relationships with other characters. Your questions and suggestions enriched Ryan's character and the whole novel.

Thank you to my colleagues and administrators at Friends

Select School and Staten Island Academy for enthusiastically supporting my writing. And to the students I have taught: Your humor and commitment to justice have inspired me, and I have great hope for our future because I know all of you.

To my family, my in-laws, and my friends who feel like family: I love you and am so touched by your excitement for my first novel. Myles and Clint, I understand Lauren's love for Ryan because of my love for both of you.

To my mom, Elizabeth Morrison: Thank you for modeling grace, compassion, and hard work. Thank you for reading everything I write and for telling me, "You *can't* stop writing," when I thought about giving up. Thank you for the countless hours you've spent with C. so I could write. I've spent years working toward the goal of getting published, but I'm still working on my most important goal: being the kind of mother you are.

To Mike: Thank you for prioritizing my writing dream and for your kindness, your humor, and your devotion to me and to us. Everything that's good is more fun because of you, and everything that's hard is more manageable. You are the best partner I could ask for. And to my strong, sweet, smart, and silly Cora: You bring me joy in every moment. May you have all of Lauren's passion and loyalty with none of her propensity for shoplifting. I love you always.

—LM

About the Authors

CORDELIA JENSEN is the author of two YA novels-in-verse: *The Way the Light Bends* and *Skyscraping*, which was named a 2016 ALA Best Book for Young Adults.

LAURIE MORRISON taught middle school for 10 years before writing *Every Shiny Thing*.

Both authors live in Philadelphia and received MFAs in writing for children and young adults from the Vermont College of Fine Arts.

The Teacher's Guide for
EVERY SHINY THING

By Cordelia Jensen and Laurie Morrison

HOW TO USE THIS GUIDE

Every Shiny Thing is a timely and relatable novel about friendship, family, and social justice. The book raises big questions that are perfect to discuss with ten -to fourteen-year-old readers. The unique format—alternating prose and verse sections—lends itself to productive and accessible discussions about novel structure, literary devices, and the poetic form. As a result, *Every Shiny Thing* is a great choice for a classroom read aloud, whole-class text, literature circle, book club, or summer reading list.

The discussion questions in this guide are rooted in the Common Core standards for language arts. The first set of questions is divided by chapter. Students can think, talk, and write about these questions as they read the book. The second set of questions is intended for use after students have finished reading the novel. Any of the questions can be adapted as analytical or reflective writing prompts.

CLASSROOM DISCUSSION QUESTIONS

LAUREN • *The Hardest Good bye*

• When we meet Lauren, she is absolutely sure that the Piedmont School is not the right place for her brother, Ryan. What are Lauren's reasons for believing that Piedmont is wrong for Ryan? Do you agree with Lauren's reasoning? Why or why not?

• How do you think Lauren and Ryan's parents feel about leaving Ryan at Piedmont, and how does Lauren think they feel? How do you know?

SIERRA • *Out of Body* to *Moving Sideways*

• When we meet Sierra, her mother has just been arrested. How does Sierra feel about her mother and about the idea of being separated from her? Find a few lines from the book that support your thinking.

• Sierra's chapters are written in verse, and some of her poems have striking spacing. Some lines are indented more than others, and sometimes there is a large space in the middle of a line. Find a place in Sierra's first section where something about the spacing strikes you. Consider what impact that spacing has on the emphasis or meaning in the poem. As you keep reading, look out for other places where the spacing strikes you.

LAUREN • *What Really Matters*

• Lauren's parents give Ryan and Lauren shiny new phones and computers. Why do they do this? So far, do you think they seem like good parents? Why or why not?

• At Lauren's first Worship and Ministry meeting, Mr. Ellis tells her that she has "a strong sense of social responsibility" (25). What does it mean to have "a strong sense of social responsibility?" What are some things that Lauren says, thinks, and does that reveal her growing interest in social justice issues?

SIERRA • *Crowding* to *Secret Room*

• Sierra's kaleidoscope is a symbol: a significant object that takes on layers of meaning. Why is the kaleidoscope important to Sierra, and what does it represent to her? Keep paying attention to kaleidoscope and color imagery throughout the novel.

• When Anne and Carl drive Sierra to her foster home, Sierra thinks,

> "They can take me
> to wherever they live
> but they can't make me
>
> theirs" (39).

Why do you think the word "theirs" is separated from the rest of the passage? What does this passage tell you about Sierra's attitude toward Anne and Carl? Why does she feel this way?

• Carl tells Sierra not to go in the room near hers, but she peeks in anyway. What predictions can you make about this room and why Anne might cry if Sierra went inside?

LAUREN • *The Scheme Team*

• Describe Lauren and Audrey's friendship. How has it changed since Ryan went away to Piedmont?

• What is Lauren's big plan? Does it seem like a good idea? Why or why not?

SIERRA • *Expressions* to *Gnaws & Wishes*

• Anne, Carl, and Lauren all try to do kind things for Sierra because they want to make Sierra feel comfortable. Describe what each of them does to welcome Sierra. Compare and contrast Sierra's reactions to their kind actions.

• Sierra uses a simile when she thinks about how her worry for her mom feels "like wearing a life jacket made of lead" (72). A simile is a comparison between two things that aren't literally the same but are similar in some important and revealing way. Similes always use the words "like" or "as." What does it mean that Sierra's worry is "like wearing a life jacket made of lead"? Why do you think Sierra feels this way about her mom? As you keep reading the book, look out for more similes.

LAUREN • *Costumes for Three*

• Lauren feels distant from her old best friend Audrey but immediately connects with Sierra. Compare and contrast Audrey and Sierra as friends for Lauren. Why does Lauren feel more comfortable with Sierra than Audrey?

• At this point in the novel, Lauren has begun to make some questionable choices that could hurt other people or get her in trouble. Make a list of any of Lauren's actions that make you uncomfortable. How does she convince herself that these actions are okay?

SIERRA • *Fates* to *Latching On*

• How does Sierra react when Audrey and Lauren get angry? Find specific lines that show how she feels and what she does when other people are mad.

• Why does it upset Sierra when Anne "assumes" and "insists" things? (100). Why does Sierra feel more comfortable with Carl than with Anne? What predictions can you make about how Sierra's relationships with Anne and Carl might change throughout the rest of the book?

LAUREN • *Partners in Justice*

• Describe what happens with the Three Fates Halloween costumes. What does this incident reveal about Audrey? Why does it make Lauren so upset?

• List the new information we learn about Ryan in this chapter. What adjectives would you use to describe Ryan and his relationship with Lauren?

• Explain why Lauren decides to tell Sierra about her plan and ask for Sierra's help. Does it surprise you that Sierra agrees? Why or why not?

SIERRA • *Mixed Up* to *Switch Places*

• In the lines quoted below, Sierra uses a metaphor. Like a simile, a metaphor is a comparison between two things that are not literally the same. Unlike a simile, a metaphor does not use the words "like" or "as." What does this metaphor reveal to you about the way Sierra feels about her friendship with Lauren and their distance from Lauren's former close friends? Where else in the novel can you find metaphors?

> "Instead I join Lauren,
> > just the two of us,
> > our own island
> > her old friends

a   churnin

sea   away." (132)

• Describe what happens when Sierra loses her temper and says something hurtful to Anne. Why do you think Sierra does this? What predictions can you make about how this moment might change Sierra and Anne's relationship?

LAUREN • *Consequences*

• Why does Lauren get so angry with her dad on the way home from her field hockey game? Do you think Lauren is right to be mad at her dad? Why or why not? Is there anything he could do or say that might make Lauren feel better?

• Lauren can tell that something is bothering Sierra, but Sierra doesn't tell Lauren what's wrong. However, we can guess what's bothering Sierra from Sierra's last chapter. When the reader knows more than a character knows it is called dramatic irony. Why is Sierra acting sad and distant, and why doesn't she tell Lauren what's going on? As you keep reading, look out for other instances of dramatic irony where you know something that one of the narrators doesn't know.

• Why does Lauren decide to keep going with her plan even after what happens with her parents? Find a passage that explains her motivation for continuing. Is Lauren's commitment to her plan admirable? Why or why not?

SIERRA • *Slide Closer* to *Yes, I Know, I Can*

• The poems in this section provide some foreshadowing (or hints) about what happened the day Sierra's mom was arrested, and Sierra's texts with her mom give us some insight about Sierra's mom's personality. Based on these clues, what can you infer about what might have happened on the day Sierra was taken away from her mom?

• Look out for moments throughout this section when Lauren says something that makes Sierra mad. Why does Sierra forgive Lauren so quickly each time? What do these moments tell you about Lauren and Sierra's friendship?

LAUREN • *Easier to Breathe*

• Juxtaposition occurs when two contrasting things are seen or placed close together. In this chapter, spot moments of juxtaposition when Lauren notices evidence of wealth and poverty back-to-back. These moments have a big impact on Lauren. Why do you think they impact her so strongly?

• Lauren is becoming more and more hooked on taking things for her plan. Find lines that suggest that Lauren is becoming addicted to stealing. If you were Lauren's friend and you knew what she was doing, what would you say to her?

SIERRA • *Shaky* to *A Little Away*

• On page 194, Anne tells Sierra that broken things can get repurposed to make something beautiful. She's talking about broken china, but how might this concept be important to the big ideas in the novel? What is "broken" in Sierra's life right now? What do you think Sierra could do to make the broken parts of her life more beautiful?

• Since Sierra is feeling conflicted about Lauren, she invites Cassidy over but ends up feeling some tension with Cassidy as well. Compare and contrast Cassidy and Lauren as friends for Sierra. In what ways are they different, and in what ways are they similar?

LAUREN • *The Best Person I Know*

• After Lauren's mom comes home from Thanksgiving with Ryan, she insists that Ryan is doing well at school. Between Ryan's latest video and Lauren's mom's descriptions, we get several pieces of evidence that suggest Ryan might be happy at Piedmont. In your opinion, which piece of evidence is most convincing? Why doesn't Lauren believe any of the evidence?

• How does Lauren react after she steals in this chapter? Why do you think she feels differently after this theft than she has felt after the others?

SIERRA • *From the Looks of It* to *Drifts*

• What does Sierra find out about Amy? Does this information surprise you? Why does it make Sierra feel guilty?

• Describe what happens when Sierra gets to see her mom. What emotions does Sierra feel during this visit? What emotions do you think her mom feels, and how can you tell?

LAUREN • *Not OK at All*

• At the Lees' party, Lauren has a flashback in which she remembers last year's party, when Ryan played the piano. Why do you think this flashback is important? What does it tell you about Ryan, Audrey, and/or Lauren?

• At the end of the chapter, why isn't Lauren OK at all? What do you think she should do at this point? What do you predict she will do?

SIERRA • *Dulled* to *Finding*

• Are you surprised by what Sierra does in the poem "Disappointment"? Do you think this is the right thing to do? Why or why not?

• Explain what Sierra realizes in the poem "Finding." What does she come to understand about how her mother, Lauren, and her fall on the bike are all related? How does this realization show a big change in her character?

LAUREN • *Restitution*

• Compare and contrast the ways Lauren's parents react to finding out what she has done.

• Which moments in this chapter make Lauren feel the worst, and why do you think those moments make her feel so badly? What do these moments tell you about Lauren?

SIERRA • *Just for Today* to *Kaleidoscope*

• How has Sierra changed from the beginning of the novel to now? Find a passage somewhere in this section that shows what she has learned and how she has grown.

LAUREN • *Something Yellow*

• What does Lauren finally realize about her parents, and what does she finally realize about Ryan? Why do you think it was so difficult for her to understand these things before?

• What do you predict will happen between Lauren and Sierra right after the last line of the novel? What will they talk about, and what will they need to do in order to make "something new" together?

BIG PICTURE DISCUSSION QUESTIONS

• What is the significance of the book's title? Can it mean different things? Can you think of any other titles that might also fit the book well?

• What are the big messages or themes of *Every Shiny Thing*? Find evidence in the text to support your ideas.

• Why do you think the authors chose to use regular, prose-style narration for Lauren's chapters and verse for Sierra's chapters? In what ways does verse fit Sierra's character and prose fit Lauren's? What was it like for you as a reader to shift between these two types of storytelling?

• Because the book has two point-of-view characters, readers get to see Lauren and Sierra from each other's perspectives. What things did you realize about Lauren from Sierra's sections that you might not have known or appreciated if you'd only gotten Lauren's point of view? What things did you realize about Sierra from Lauren's sections that you might not have known or appreciated If you'd only gotten Sierra's point of view?

• Sierra's kaleidoscope is an important symbol: a significant object that takes on layers of meaning. Think about the times she refers to the kaleidoscope and its colors throughout the novel and what happens to the kaleidoscope by the end. What does the kaleidoscope reveal about Sierra, the way she sees the world, and the way she grows? What other objects in the novel might be symbols?

• What does it mean to be a good friend? In what ways are Lauren and Sierra good friends to each other? In what ways do they let each other down?

• It's important to Lauren to be a good sister to Ryan, and it's important to Sierra to be a good daughter to her mom. In what ways is Lauren a good sister, and in what ways is Sierra a good daughter? Are Lauren's and

Sierra's ideas about what it means to be a good sister and daughter misguided in any ways? If so, how?

• Lauren makes some pretty bad decisions because she is determined to do something good. Which of her actions made you most uncomfortable and why? Is it ever okay to break rules if you have good intentions and might be able to do something positive? Why or why not?

• Consider the messages about addiction in this novel. What is an addiction? Which characters struggle with different kinds of addiction? What does the novel suggest about what a person should do if they are close to someone who has an addiction?

• Consider the roles of parents and foster parents in the novel. Are Lauren and Ryan's parents good parents, in your opinion? What do they do to support and show their love for their kids, and what mistakes do they make? Are Anne and Carl "excellent foster parents," as Sierra's caseworker tells Sierra? What do they do to support and show their love for Sierra, and what mistakes do they make? Even though Sierra's mom and dad have made big mistakes, they have also shown their love for her. What positive things have they done for Sierra?

Read on for a sneak peak at
Laurie Morrison's new book

Chapter 1

The loudest kind of quiet filled the classroom. Pens scratched paper, erasers squeaked, and desk legs groaned as the clock on the wall *tick-tick-tick*ed. Faster and faster, it seemed, even though Annabelle knew that was impossible.

She was almost out of time.

And the thing was, she got *extra* time. She and the four other seventh graders with "learning accommodations" got forty-five minutes longer than the rest of the kids, who'd already pushed in their chairs and turned in their exam booklets and burst into the hallways to celebrate the start of summer. But forty-five extra minutes didn't do Annabelle any good when her brain had gone as hazy as the harbor on a foggy day.

She ran her fingertip across the skinny blue lines in

the booklet where she was supposed to be writing her essay. The essay that counted for 25 percent of the history exam grade, as Mr. Derrickson had told them over and over. She traced one, two, three lines across the page and wished she were staring down at the thick black lines along the bottom of the pool.

She didn't need those black lines to guide her from one end of the pool to the other anymore. Her body always stayed straight, and she knew exactly how many strokes to take before it was time to flip underwater and push off the wall, propelling herself back the other way. But she still liked knowing they were there, as familiar as everything else about swimming. The glint of sunlight on the pool's pale blue surface. The mingled scents of sunscreen, chlorine, and greasy snack bar food. The splash of diving in and the cool welcome of the water.

The learning specialist, Ms. Ames, put her hand on Annabelle's wrist.

"Just write down anything you remember, okay?" she whispered. "Like we talked about. That way Mr. Derrickson can give you credit for what you know."

So Annabelle took three deep breaths, the way she always did before a race, and tried to tune out the clock's echoing tick and the other kids' frantic writing.

She managed to fill up half the page . . . but she knew

exactly what Mr. Derrickson would do when he read what she'd written. He'd scrawl question marks in the margins with his green pen. He'd write, "Irrelevant," and "Please answer the question," and "Where is your thesis?"

She flipped through the rest of the test. All those multiple-choice questions with all those choices that sounded right. The fill-in-the-blank section Mr. Derrickson had insisted was "easy-peasy." "Automatic points for anybody who's studied at all." Right.

"Okay," Ms. Ames said from the front of the room. "Put your pens and pencils down, please. And congratulations! You're officially done with seventh grade!"

Two kids whooped and high-fived each other. Annabelle looked at the essay she'd barely started, barely holding back tears as she gathered up her things.

She managed to echo Ms. Ames's "Have a good summer" before stumbling into the hallways that had emptied out almost an hour ago. When Mia and Jeremy and everyone else had all gone to lunch without her.

The other four extra-time kids were all boarding students, so they told Annabelle they'd see her at middle school closing ceremonies and headed to the cafeteria or the dorms. Annabelle pushed open the side door, stepping into the bright June sunshine.

She gulped in the island air—a little bit salty if you

really paid attention, even this far from the ocean. It was over, anyway. Seventh grade was finally done, and summer stretched out ahead of her, full of adventures with Mia and Jeremy and summer swim team practices at the pool, where most of the kids didn't go to the Academy and she got to be Annabelle the star butterflyer, not Annabelle who could never finish her work on time at school.

Mom's car was waiting at the curb, and she rolled down the window. "Belle! How'd it go, honey? Did we study the right things? Did you feel ready?"

"I'm never ready for Mr. Derrickson's tests."

Annabelle plopped down onto the hot front seat, tossed her things on the floor, and slammed the door closed.

Mom's eyebrows folded in, forming that tiny worry line right in the middle. That was how she used to look at Dad, back when things got really bad. And it was how she looked at Annabelle now, way, way too often.

"Well, you worked so hard," Mom said. "I'm sure all that effort paid off."

Then she nodded. As if she could nod those words into being true. She patted Annabelle's knee and reached up to grip the steering wheel, her silver bracelets clinking. Mitch had given her one of those bracelets for each of their wedding anniversaries. She had three so far, and she wore them all the time.

"Where to?" she asked as she pulled away from the curb. "My next meeting isn't until two. We could go out for a special lunch. Do you want to call Mitch to see if he's free? I know he'll want to celebrate with you, too."

Annabelle watched out the window as they drove along the school's winding driveway, past dorms and fields and high school kids who sat on the grass, laughing as they signed each other's yearbooks. Past the gray-shingled office where they'd come for her admissions interview two years ago—the summer before sixth grade, when she and Mom and Mitch had first moved to Gray Island.

The Academy was a boarding school, mostly, for sixth- to twelfth-grade students from the mainland. But Mom had read on their website that they "strive to be a community school" and set aside financial aid for "qualified day students" who live on the island. So she'd filled out an application for Annabelle, and somehow Annabelle had gotten in.

Because barely any other island kids had applied, probably. Because most island kids thought everybody at the Academy was snobby.

"You must be hungry, huh?" Mom said.

She was, but if they went out to lunch in town, Mom and Mitch would know everybody and everybody would ask about school because that's what everybody *always* asked about. And anyway, after this morning, her whole body ached with the need to swim.

"Actually can you drop me off at the pool?" she asked. "I can eat there."

"But you don't have practice today," Mom pointed out.

"Yeah, but we did yesterday," Annabelle reminded her, as if she needed to be reminded. "And I really need to swim today, since I skipped it."

Mom had made Annabelle stay home from summer team practice to squeeze in a few more hours of studying, not that those extra hours had done any good.

Mom sighed, and Annabelle sort of wished Mitch had been the one to pick her up. Mitch would have agreed to take her to the pool in an instant because he *got* it—how important it was for Annabelle to train. How good she was, and how great she could be.

"You probably have lots of work anyway, right?" Annabelle said. "With all the summer people wanting you to plan all their parties? Could we do takeout from Lombardi's tonight instead? I'm in a gnocchi mood."

Mom hesitated at the stop sign, but she turned left instead of right, toward the pool instead of back to town. Annabelle's shoulders relaxed for the first time since she'd sat down to start her test that morning.

"All right, Belle. You deserve to celebrate how you want. The pool and Lombardi's it is."

Mom probably wouldn't feel that way if she'd seen how little Annabelle had written for her essay, but Annabelle kept her mouth shut and watched all the giant vacation homes they passed, mostly occupied again now that summer was finally starting.

When they got to the pool, Mom said the same exact things she always did: to be safe and reapply sunscreen and drink plenty of water. Then she leaned over to give Annabelle an extra-tight, extra-long hug.

"I'll come back to get you after my two o'clock meeting," she said into Annabelle's ear. "And, hey. I'm proud of you no matter what. You know that, right?"

Annabelle nodded as she pulled away from Mom's hug and then stepped out of the car. But did that even count, the kind of pride you didn't have to do anything good to earn?

The story continues in *Up for Air*
by Laurie Morrison